By the same author
Calling All Monsters
He Came from the Shadows

• CHRIS WESTWOOD •

SHOCK WAVES

CLARION BOOKS · NEW YORK

Clarion Books
a Houghton Mifflin Company imprint
215 Park Avenue South, New York, NY 10003
Text copyright © 1992 by Chris Westwood

Library of Congress Cataloging-in-Publication Data
Westwood, Chris.
Shock waves / by Chris Westwood.
p. cm.
Summary: A letter from a dating service links eighteen-
year-old Leigh with the mysterious deaths of two other
college students who seem to have had the life drained from
them.
ISBN 0–395–63111–4
[1. Horror stories.] I. Title.
PZ7.W5274Sh 1992
[Fic] — dc20 91–42777
CIP
AC

AGM 10 9 8 7 6 5 4 3 2 1

This book is for many friends, for many reasons:

Mike Barber and Elaine Graham, Julian Richards,
Craig K. McCall, Karen Short and Jim McWhinney,
Karol and Clare Cioma, Mark Talbot-Butler . . .

All were there in Bournemouth when it mattered,
and it won't go unnoticed that the Technical College
described in the story doesn't really exist,
except as a hybrid of other colleges.
Hopefully Bournemouth and Poole will also forgive
my taking liberties with their streets and beaches . . .
all in the cause of fiction. But everything else
here is for real, believe me.

SHOCK
WAVES

· 1 ·

The killer was on the loose again.

Not that anyone at the party he'd gate-crashed tonight was aware of that. Since early evening, guests at the opulent white house on Pinewood Road, Branksome Park, had grown steadily less and less sober while the killer moved among them, unnoticed, and he'd long ago mastered the art of blending in. Now, wandering from one spacious white room to another, sidestepping couples who were seated cross-legged on the floor, he nodded and smiled as others nodded and smiled at him. In the center of what must have been the dining room stood a working marble fountain, especially lit up for the occasion.

Some people, he thought.

Perhaps the building had been a hotel once. There were Vacancies signs elsewhere in the street, and the well-tended swimming pool at the rear seemed the kind of detail that might have drawn vacationers. There was no moon tonight, but lights from the house caused the surface of the kidney-shaped pool to gleam brightly. Several unattached girls sat around it, drinking, pretending not to notice him watching. The water looked fathomless as sleep without dreams. As he stood there, staring, drifting, the sound of waves filled the killer's mind.

The girl he'd half hoped to find here had been indoors all along. He hadn't set out purposely to find her, but there was always the chance that he would. She was in one of the quieter rooms, where no music played and guests perched on beanbags and comfortable chairs. She stood by a print of one of Hockney's swimming pools: a splash left by a diver. Her long dark hair and hazel eyes reminded him of someone he'd once seen playing Ophelia in *Hamlet*. He couldn't remember whether that had been in a film or onstage. Even her dress, which came down to her shins and was covered with print flowers in delicate faded colors, reminded him of Ophelia.

Still, her appearance was only the half of it: in all his years he'd never judged anyone by looks alone. It was what he saw in her eyes when she noticed him standing there that told him it had to be her.

The snag was that someone else had already found her; she was with a boy of about her own age, eighteen perhaps, well-groomed, in beige chinos and a baggy tropical short-sleeved shirt.

Hello, he mouthed at the girl, not actually speaking the word, not needing to, but fixing her gaze from a distance of perhaps twenty feet and concluding his pass with a smile. There was no time to waste.

At first she must have wondered what to make of him, and she turned her face away. The well-groomed boy talked on, but she didn't digest a word he was saying. She nodded and sipped whatever pink fizz was in the glass she held, and tried to smile, and glanced again at the killer.

It was love at first sight, no doubt about it.

Hello, the killer mouthed again. It's me: the one you've been waiting for.

Such magic in the air tonight, he thought, such changes in the climate. It was late April, certainly one of the warmest April nights on record, and it felt like the onset of summer madness. There was heat in the room, and just because the others hadn't noticed didn't mean it wasn't there.

Then, before the boy knew what was happening, the girl —his date! how dare she!—had pushed her glass into his hand and marched smartly away. Watching her go, his face changed markedly as the light dawned. He stood as if hand-cuffed, a glass in each hand. His first thought must have been that she was heading for the toilets. Then she was linking arms with the killer and leaving the room.

"Hey!" His voice sounded startled, pitched high as a girl's. "Hey, you! What do you think you're—"

"Hello," said the killer to the girl. "Do you know me?"

"Hello," said the girl. "I don't think so, but I get the feeling I'm going to."

The spell had fallen. There was romance in the air, and the night was dreamless, its soundtrack all soft distant music and near-silent waves. As they headed outdoors toward the pool, the boy came panting up behind them, seizing the killer's right arm to spin him around. The girl turned with him, her flat shoes skidding slightly on the tiles at the pool's edge.

"What's going on here?" the boy demanded, fists bunching at the ready. Several of the unattached girls looked up with expectant faces. "She's with me. You'd better get moving, fella."

"That's fine with me," the killer said, turning away again, the girl still clinging on for dear life. "Watch me go. I'm moving already."

"Isabelle!" The boy's voice was cracking now, a shout that for a second made the party seem to have fallen silent around him. "Come back here now! You don't even know this cretin!" Perhaps spurred by the sound of his own voice, the boy lunged forward again.

This time the killer flashed out his free right arm, quick as a drawn sword, and then the boy was toppling aside, hitting the water with a smack. There was a frozen moment like Hockney's painting, a longer, extended moment as the boy went under, ripples forming out of waves, and the unattached girls at the poolside sucked in their breath as if to avoid drowning too. By the time the boy surfaced, spitting out water, the killer had the girl halfway to his car.

· 2 ·

The letter arrived first thing on Monday. Leigh Taylor, already ten minutes late, collected it almost without seeing it from the dusty mahogany stand in the hall, and fitted it down in her bag as she shouldered open the apartment building's front door.

It was forgotten as soon as she stepped outdoors. Each morning, without exception, the sunlight on the forecourt came as a shock after the darkness in her apartment, which was tucked beneath the eaves on the wrong side of the building. Sunlight never reached there. Even if she sat at the table near the large rear window at midday, she wouldn't see her sketchbook for shadows. No wonder Sophie, who'd kept the apartment before her, referred to it as the Coffin. Already, before summer even came, the place was a sweatbox, with a bed, a two-burner hot plate and a gas heater squeezed into a ten-by-twelve space that felt like a punishment she had to endure. If she bided her time, though, someone might vacate one of the larger, more comfortable places downstairs to make room for her.

Across the forecourt, three indistinct figures waited inside a blue Citroën that rattled as its engine turned over. Sophie was at the wheel, her eyes hidden behind shades as though she were recovering from one more heavy night. The other figures were mere blurs until Leigh climbed in and saw Darren, with whom Sophie had been living since the start of the semester, and Joan, from the apartment beneath her own. The Cowboy Junkies distorted through speakers directly behind Leigh's head.

"Did you think to pick up your mail?" Joan said to Leigh, and Sophie said, "Glad to see you made it. We were starting to think you were still asleep. I hit the horn three times, didn't I, Darren?"

"Mondays are always the worst," Joan said. This morning she looked like living proof of that, her black hair an unwashed maze, her skin so pale, she must have been missing sleep. "God, why don't I go back to bed?" she wondered.

Leigh smiled to herself as Sophie jerked and jumped the Citroën onto Cavendish Road, where the gutters were colorfully thick with dead leaves left over from winter. "Seems I missed one of those nights again."

"Weren't you there?" Joan frowned, touching her forehead with her fingertips. "Then again, where was *I*? And who with? Hope I didn't do anything I'll regret later."

"You usually do," Sophie said. "Old habits die hard."

As they turned left onto Lansdowne Road, a blaze of blue lights flashed toward the Citroën, then past—two police cars and an ambulance heading down into Bournemouth. The vehicles were just out of sight when their sirens began.

Joan leaned forward from the rear, brandishing a spent roll of 35mm film. "Darren, be a love and put this through processing with yours. I won't have time—I'm supposed to be meeting Graham tonight."

Darren pushed the film deep into his backpack.

"And was Graham there last night?" Sophie asked, forgetting the road as she twisted to look at Joan. "Then no wonder you don't remember what happened; just knew he'd have something to do with it."

"Mind your own damn business," Joan replied. Her eyes, when she glanced at Leigh, were bloodshot and tired. "Don't dare take Graham's name in vain, Sophie, I'm warning you. Talk about him and you're treading on hallowed ground." Wincing, again touching her temples to soothe the pain, she added quietly, "Ouch, I think I'm in love."

"Looks like it," Leigh said, a little too loudly, since the music had stopped. "Maybe we'll meet him sometime."

Sophie gave a theatrical laugh. "She's keeping him all to herself, Leigh. He must be too sensitive to mix with plebs like us. We'd break his fragile shell." Sometimes it was difficult to tell Sophie's jests and poison gibes apart. "Really, Joan. You should introduce us. You can't keep him hidden forever."

"I know," Joan said. "I was going to, soon. Really I was."

"Like hell you were. You probably told him you had no friends."

It was far too early in the day for this, Leigh thought. What she needed was a silent, funereal drive to college, not Sophie's empty chatter.

Although this was only Leigh's third semester, the scene felt like something she'd lived through for years. Strangely, the evidence of hangovers she saw in the others, their good-morning grouchiness, were things she had warmed to and imagined she'd miss when the time came. They made her feel part of something, an accepted member of the circle. Initially, landing in Bournemouth without a friend to her name, she'd doubted she'd ever make one.

She had met Joan—and the others through Joan—during her first few weeks at the Tech, when most new students had been allotted rooms in local hotels by the college's student liaison officer. To begin with the accommodation system had helped socially; even shy students had been forced into getting to know others, whether or not they wanted to. But within a month Joan had tired of subsidized hotel meals, the greasy fried breakfasts and cold congealed suppers, and had joined Sophie at Silverwood Dene, where at least, she'd said, she could eat what she wanted when she wanted and didn't have to line up for the bathroom. When Sophie deserted the Coffin to share with Darren just after Christmas, Leigh had gladly moved in.

The Tech was a new, bland, gray box in the wilderness that was Wallisdown Road, between Bournemouth and Poole. This morning, with the sky piercing and cloudless and the sun causing the bare tawny landscape around the site to shimmer, the Tech appeared quieter than usual. The parking lot, an unfinished rectangle of mud and gravel behind the main building, was half empty. No students or staff rushed to and from entrances, bobbed past windows indoors. Leigh glanced briefly at Joan, but Joan seemed to have noticed none of this.

"Are we early or is someone on strike again?" Darren said, leaning far back in the passenger seat and extending both arms in a stretch. "Were we supposed to be protesting about something today?"

Nearing the main entrance, Leigh saw that there was activity of a kind in the foyer just beyond the wedged-open doors. Thirty to forty students were gathered there, milling about, most wearing faces miles long. Still pinned to the walls and the two large bulletin boards were flyers for last week's meeting in the student union bar. Leigh hadn't attended, but she knew what had been said: a second-year graphics student had been assaulted on her way home from college the previous Friday evening, and police were for the moment advising female students not to walk to or from the site alone. At the meeting there had been talk of a self-imposed curfew, shortening college hours, ot at least refusing to attend evening lectures until there was proof that the threat had passed.

"What's this all about?" Darren wondered, but the meeting already looked as if it was breaking up. Some students were walking away past the main office marked Reception, past the displays of Foundation Art and Design abstract paintings. Other groups stood talking in whispers, shaking their heads, gazing blankly into space.

"Did we miss anything important?" Leigh began saying to no one in particular. But as she did so, a burly red-faced youth pelted past her, almost through her, and ran out toward the parking lot as if his life depended upon haste. Had he been crying, or was that just the impression he'd given in his panting hurry? She turned back to the others, shrugging.

"Something happening?" Sophie demanded of a second-year girl whom Leigh didn't know but recognized. The girl, a student-union rep wearing army fatigues with stitched-on Campaign for Nuclear Disarmament badges on the sleeves, shook her head with a pale, exhausted expression.

"Something already has," she replied.

Out in the parking lot a vehicle driven by the red-faced youth reversed, clashed gears, accelerated away with a screech like a cheap effect in a cop film.

"I don't see as he can do any good," the girl said. "He'll only make things worse for himself."

If it hadn't been for the general aura of shock in the foyer, Leigh would have guessed that what was happening here was political. She was about to ask again when the girl said, "Do any of you know Isabelle Brooks? Second year Art and Design. That was her boyfriend leaving just now." The name was one Leigh knew. She remembered seeing the couple together at breaks.

"Well, if any of you saw her lately, you're to tell the police," the student rep finished, turning away. "They fished her out of Poole Harbor this morning."

· 3 ·

Years ago—Leigh would have been pushed to recall exactly when—there had been a repeat TV showing of *The Prisoner,* a cult 1960s series that began, each week, with a jet of knockout gas issuing in through Patrick McGoohan's keyhole until the world turned sideways, then faded out completely. McGoohan awoke, later, in a strange Mediterranean village like the scene of a surrealist's nightmare. In an instant, his world had changed.

Of course she'd been too young when *The Prisoner* was broadcast to remember anything now but stray details: the vast white bubble named Rover rising from the sea with a roar to pursue and apprehend anyone who dared try escaping the village; an observation chamber complete with video screens from which any resident could be spied upon at any time.

For some reason, the whole of this Monday morning seemed touched by the image of that gas turning everything hazy. Not that she or anyone else in college had been zapped;

just that it seemed the news of Isabelle Brooks, like the gas coming in, had transformed everything forever.

Now and then, while she stood at her easel in the life class trying to capture the anemic, middle-aged model in charcoal, her focus shifted, the studio and everything in it seeming to withdraw from her. For a moment the model, reclining nude on a mattress in front of a shorting-out electric heater, became a torso slumped on a pathologist's slab. The easels drawn toward her became screens dividing the living from the dead. And at once the hush was unbearable, the unmoving white figure and the deadly scrape of pencils and charcoal sticks on paper too much to bear. Leigh would have cried out to end it, or feigned a coughing fit, at least to make sure the model was alive, if she hadn't felt Sophie's hand on her shoulder first.

"I can't believe it," Sophie said dimly. "I really can't believe it."

"Nor me," Leigh said. "Nor me."

In the cafeteria, first break, Leigh sat with her banana-shaped bag on the table before her and watched the students grouped at other tables, some smoking and borrowing smokes, exchanging odd words. Not many were lost in conversation. Heads were still shaking, barely perceptibly, in disbelief at the news. Last week's student meeting and talk of curfews had been meant to wake people up to the dangers waiting outside, but who had been ready for this?

"It seems so personal, that's what's so awful," Sophie was saying. "When you read about things like this in the papers and it's someone you never knew, you never feel so affected. But this is too close, someone you're going to notice not being around. . . . " She tailed off, dropping her elbows on the table, resting her chin on her knuckled hands.

"Did you know her?" Leigh said.

"Only to say hello to. I knew she had a bit of a reputation, but you wouldn't think—"

"Reputation?" Leigh asked quizzically. At the same time, a commotion began somewhere behind her: someone was rocking and punching the coffee machine, which presumably had eaten their change. Then Sophie said, "Look, here's Joan."

Leigh turned just in time to see Joan deliver one last kick to the coffee machine before striding toward their table like a vision of darkness—wild black hair, oversized leather bomber jacket, drainpipe jeans that made her legs impossibly long and elegant. She could have been a true beauty if she'd tried, Leigh thought. If anything, she looked worse now, more emaciated, than she had that morning in the car.

"What're you *on*, Joan?" Leigh wondered aloud.

"Huh?"

"Doesn't matter."

Frowning, Joan scraped a spare chair back from the table and collapsed haphazardly onto it. Her Nikon camera bumped and dangled in sympathy on her chest. Of the girls in Leigh's circle, Joan was the only one taking Photography instead of Art and Design. Darren was also taking the photography course. Joan's specialties were bleak landscapes, barren coastlines, condemned buildings, though her heart was set on a future in the music press.

"Are you managing to focus your enlarger this morning?" Sophie asked now.

"If that's supposed to be funny," Joan said, and then managed a shrug and a smile. "Sorry. Haven't been sleeping too well. You know how it is to be in love, though, don't you?"

Leigh wasn't sure that she did. "If that's what it does to you, I'm probably better off out of it."

"Whoever I'm with," Sophie said, absently marking invisible circles on the tabletop with her forefinger, "I always tell myself it's love . . . while it lasts. And afterward I know it wasn't at all, not really. Just a passing phase."

Joan's eyes narrowed. "Are you saying this is a phase *I'm* going through?"

"Not necessarily. Only that you can't always tell, even when you think you can."

"And now that you're with Darren, you can tell that's love?"

"Oh, of course. No question about it."

Joan snorted laughter, which quickly spread to the others. For a moment everything became normal again, the atmosphere lighter. The relief didn't last, however. In Sophie's face, then in Joan's, Leigh detected something beneath the good humor; traces of the fear and disbelief that had silenced the rest of the college that day.

"It's such a terrible thing," Joan said without prompting. "I still can't believe what I've heard. Did they say whether or not it was an accident?"

"No one knows anything," Leigh said.

"Not even how it happened," Sophie said. "All we know is where they found her. And it's easy to speculate over things we don't know about, but none of it helps. It even seems, well, *disrespectful* somehow. Have you got the time, Leigh?"

"And maybe some change," Joan said, brightening suddenly. "If I could borrow some change until I've broken this note, I might stand a chance with that coffee machine again."

"Ten forty." Leigh said, unzipping her bag, fishing inside for her purse.

As she did, Joan casually snatched at something in the midst of Leigh's bag. "What's this? Something from your own secret love?"

She was holding the letter that had arrived that morning. It was still unopened, and now for the first time Leigh noticed how tidily scripted the handwritten address was, and what the sender had done to her name. LEIGH MONDRIAN TAYLOR, it read.

"Well!" Joan said, returning the envelope.

"Well. Are you sure *you* don't know what it is?" Leigh said, and then to Sophie, "Or you?"

"Meaning what?"

"That no one else I know uses Mondrian, or Picasso, or Degas when they write to me." Her gaze was fixed on Joan as she spoke. Joan lifted her hands, palms up, in a plea of innocence. "When we went to the Tate last year, you were with me when I bought those Mondrian postcards. You know he's my favorite artist."

Joan shrugged. "But this isn't my handwriting. In any case, does it really matter? Aren't you going to open it?"

As she tore at the sealed envelope, Leigh smiled confidently first at Joan, then Sophie. "If this turns out to be a gushing love letter, I'll know who's responsible for sending it. I don't care whose handwriting it's in."

She hesitated while several students at one of the other

tables rose slowly to leave the cafeteria like mourners departing a grave. They seemed to have taken the news about Isabelle badly; perhaps they were—had been—friends of hers. When they'd gone, Leigh removed from the envelope two sheets of photocopied paper, flattening them out on the table. It took her a moment or two to gauge what they were.

The first sheet was headed notepaper. Apollo Introductions, it said. Beneath the return address, a local one, her name—"Dear Leigh"—had been written in the same careful hand as on the envelope. The rest was a printed form letter, which, before she'd had a chance to digest it, Sophie had snatched up and started to read, eyes widening as she did. The second sheet was a questionnaire. Did she live alone? Did she have an active social life? What were her interests?

"Really, Leigh," Sophie exclaimed, and passed the letter toward Joan. "A dating agency! Well, you are a dark horse! Did you really send off for that?"

"No, but one of you did."

"And if we told you we had nothing to do with this?"

"I'd still find it hard to believe."

Joan shook her head, smiling broadly, not bothering to read the letter in her hands. For the first time today she was brightening; a familiar spark of mischief had returned to her eye. "But you're going to reply to it, aren't you? It says you have to be over eighteen, but they don't ask for proof: you can easily fake it. It could be exactly what you need. It's time something brought a little passion to your life!"

"Isn't it time *you* were back in the darkroom?" Leigh said, pointing the way. "Haven't you prints to develop?"

"Not until I've attacked the coffee machine again."

"So what will you do?" Sophie was saying to Leigh. "Will you reply? What do you think?"

"What do I think?" In one quick motion, Leigh seized both sheets of paper together with their envelope and crumpled the lot between her fists, tossing the paper ball over her shoulder like salt for good luck. "That's what I think. I can manage quite well without this sort of help, thanks. I don't need computers to fix me up."

"But it doesn't say a word about computers," Sophie said. "In fact, it makes it quite clear—" But Leigh's look stopped her short, told her the joke was over. "All right, we'll say no more about it. But believe me, this didn't come from me."

• • •

After all, she had no reason to doubt their word; in any case, why should they lie? In the end, it really didn't matter one way or another; the circular was only someone's harmless joke at her expense. Of course, she had never known anyone the way Sophie knew Darren or Joan apparently knew Graham, but so what? She wasn't so desperate, and what you'd never had you never missed. There was no need to dwell on it, no need to let the letter fill her thoughts through the rest of the day, as it did.

The dreadful news about Isabelle was what had made her edgy, she decided, for she couldn't believe the dating agency's solicitation could have upset her so badly. But by the time her last class of the day was ending—a three-hour session of still-life drawing—her mind was filling with another image: a crushed paper ball discarded on the cafeteria floor.

There were no late lectures on Mondays. As she and Sophie emerged from their studio, they found Joan outside, yawning.

"Where's Darren?" Sophie wanted to know, but Joan could only shrug and say, "I haven't seen him all day."

"Well, he can make his own way home for once. I'm not in the mood for waiting."

Outside, the light was thickening. Together they trudged toward the Citroën. Halfway across the parking lot Leigh stopped and turned back. "Wait for me. I won't be a minute. I just need the ladies'."

Seconds later, she found herself standing just inside the rest room nearest the cafeteria, breathing deeply, astonished by the pounding of her heart. Her reflected face above the washbasin looked properly guilty for having lied: she hadn't intended to use the bathroom at all. She'd ducked in here only to calm herself, but what was she worried about?

The cafeteria itself was empty. The tables had been cleared and sponged, all dirty plastic cups and empty potato-chip bags swept clean. For no reason she knew of, Leigh suddenly felt like a criminal, creeping secretly about where she shouldn't be.

Rounding the coffee machine, which stood flush to the wall near the door, she noticed wrappers and cigarette butts beneath some of the tables where the cleaners had missed. Still, there was no sign of the paper ball she'd flung away earlier. Perhaps it hadn't been meant for her to keep after all.

· 4 ·

Joan came up to the Coffin while Leigh was still toweling her hair from the shower. Squeezing inside the dim room, she made a face and took a seat at the table by the window.

"How can you stand it? This place is a sauna, for crying out loud."

"I used one of the burners on the hot plate an hour ago," Leigh told her. "It's what they call heat efficient."

"Feels like too much of a good thing," Joan said. "You should complain to O'Reilly. If he can't get you something better, he at least ought to get you a cold-air fan."

"I'd rather not see him unless it's really necessary." Leigh shrugged.

Joan peered through the darkness under the eaves toward more darkness beyond. The night was peaceful except for the rustle of close-planted birch trees behind the house. "I know what you mean. He's so full of himself and so silky, who'd trust him? I wouldn't be surprised if he spent his nights in the local underpasses, lifting his raincoat at passersby."

Leigh might have found that amusing, except she could imagine it too. O'Reilly, the landlord, had an unnerving way of looking her up and down as though auditioning her whenever she went to pay rent. She put on the kettle and was rinsing out two stained mugs when Joan said, "Oh, almost forgot. I brought you this." From the depths of her jacket she drew a cracked and creased envelope. Setting it down on the table, she smoothed her palm over it and pushed it toward Leigh.

"*You,*" Leigh said. "You don't give up easily, do you? So you went back for the paper ball."

Joan smiled knowingly. "Didn't you?"

"Beg your pardon?"

"Oh, come on, Leigh, don't be so stuffy. You're easier to see through than you think, you know. You didn't go back for the ladies' tonight, did you? Besides which, sooner or later you would've been kicking yourself for throwing this away. The least you can do is let it sit here for a day or two and *then* decide what you want."

"God, you're impossible. I'm not really so desperate, you know."

Nevertheless, Leigh felt strangely relieved at the sight of the envelope, as if a door she'd thought sealed forever had mysteriously reopened. "But isn't this just junk mail? A rip-off like all the others? How do I know it'll make any difference?"

"You don't, but the trick is in finding out." Joan fell silent as she watched Leigh studiously pouring tea into mugs. "Every night you come up to this trap alone while everyone else is living it up, and every morning you leave it with that— that look in your eyes."

"What look?"

"You know. Or perhaps you don't. It's just that you seem so alone sometimes, so empty. You need to meet someone, that's what you need. It's high time you did."

"Well, thanks for being so honest," Leigh said, though she couldn't feel grateful, only vulnerable. A stable, happy love life was something she imagined happened only to others, like death or good fortune. Her last fling—her only one, really, and more a flop than a fling—had been two years ago at high school with a senior named Adrian, who had ditched her for an older girl without explanation, without so much as a fond farewell. Ridiculous though it was, she still felt a tightness inside when she thought of it, still blamed Adrian for the mess she'd made of her final exams. Could that be all that was stopping her now? The fear of being hurt again?

She could feel Joan's eyes on her as she set the mugs on the table and picked up the envelope. "If you really had nothing to do with this, why make such an issue of it?"

She'd barely got the question out when the buzzer above the door sounded. In the confined space the noise was painful, far larger than the room. Joan instinctively cupped her hands to her ears, widening her lips in a mockery of a scream. Her lips were cracked and blue and her skin so bloodless, the scream seemed to suit her, Leigh thought.

Then, before she could wonder why she should think that, the buzzer went again. She hurried from the room and along the dark corridor, downstairs, where the aroma of Indian food always seemed to hang in the air. At the top of the stairs descending to the hall was a mahogany balustrade, matching the banister on the stairs and the mail stand below. She stopped and rested her hands on it and peered down toward the front door, where two ghostly figures shifted in the night beyond the frosted glass. Before she'd even reached the door or swung it wide, she knew who the visitors were. What she didn't expect was the look on their faces, Darren's mouth open but wordless, Sophie's eyes glazed by aftershock. For a long moment she could only stand in the doorway, staring back numbly.

"Mind if we come in?" Sophie said.

"It's Isabelle Brooks," Darren began as soon as they'd reached the Coffin and settled. He spoke with a heaviness that was unusual for him. "We just found out what happened to her. All I can say is, I wish we hadn't."

• • •

With four crammed into the room, Leigh had to wedge the door open to aid the air flow. Condensation formed on the windowpane and on the vinyl wallpaper above the sink. She took a seat at the table facing Joan while Darren and Sophie sprawled on the bed. Darren held a rolled-up newspaper he'd brought and was thumping it lightly, absently against his thigh.

"I was down in Poole today," he said. "Since Christmas I've been in touch with a reporter on the *Echo,* Dave Hunt. He's been giving me a taste of journalism, letting me shoot the odd pic for the paper, just run-of-the-mill stuff, flower shows, lost and found puppies.

"So this morning I phoned, as I do every Monday, and asked if there was anything for me this week. And he sort of said, Not today—I've got something on. Turned out he'd been assigned to do a piece on Isabelle Brooks. They got the news at the *Echo* just before we did. 🐟

"What I did then was I loaded my camera and went down to the harbor, to see what was happening. There was no sign of Dave—he'd been and gone by then—but there were still a few police, and one or two others from the Tech, there for the thrill. At first, when I tried to find out what was up, the cops got suspicious, but after I'd mentioned the *Echo,* they left me alone to mill about.

"I took a few shots around the harbor. Johnny Cross was down there asking questions. He was all hot and bothered, and you could tell he'd been crying from the marks around his eyes and cheeks."

"Isabelle's ex?" Leigh wondered, and Sophie said curtly, "The one who stormed past us this morning."

Darren nodded. "We've all seen him hanging around college with Isabelle. He was especially upset because they'd split just a few days before. So he'd been trying to get his head around *that* when he heard what had happened this morning. I asked if he hoped she hadn't done anything stupid because of him."

"Would she have?" Joan wanted to know. "Was she so unbalanced she'd jump in?"

"Maybe—but from all accounts she'd probably swim straight out again. If she did something like that, it would probably be for show. He explained how her moods would fluctuate; hot one minute, lukewarm the next. Sometimes she'd drink too much; sometimes she'd pop whatever pills she could find. And he'd thought that's what she was going through, another one of her phases. She'd told him she never wanted to see him again, but apparently she sounded off like that all the time. Sure he was upset, but they'd been through it before, so he knew the pattern. She'd leave him, take up with someone else for a few days, paint the town red, and then she'd come back, cap in hand."

"Is that what you meant by her reputation?" Leigh said to Sophie. "That she played the field? She didn't like to feel tied? She'd put herself out for anyone?"

"Well," said Sophie, "I don't believe she behaved like that out of spite. She wasn't taking anyone for granted, or even meaning to do what she did. I think she was just unstable; looking for love wherever she could find it."

Darren was nodding in agreement. "This kid, Johnny, he told me she was simply confused. She'd had one of those childhoods like something in a Dickens novel: lost her parents when she was young, was brought up by relatives who'd turned out not to want her after all, wandered into various relationships with boys that ended badly. She was basically insecure, and no wonder. But he wouldn't believe she had it in her to commit suicide."

"Which leaves two possibilities: an accident of some kind," Sophie said gravely, "or murder."

For a matter of seconds the word seemed to hang in the air like smoke. Leigh shifted uneasily in her seat; a bird beat its wings furiously just above her window.

"Then which is it?" Joan said. "Is that what you came here to tell us?"

"We really don't know," Darren said, "and from what I hear, nor do the authorities. The simple fact is, accidents like this don't happen. And people who find themselves murdered don't wind up like Isabelle Brooks."

He paused and took a deep breath, and Leigh noticed the tremor that ran through him, the way his hands shook.

He went on, "Johnny Cross had brought his car down to

Poole, and when we heard they'd taken Isabelle to the nearest hospital, he offered to drive me there.

"We weren't allowed to see her, of course, but they did let us wait. No one paid us any attention. Dave Hunt was already there, flitting back and forth, trying to pick up information. There were several other reporters too, I don't know who or from what papers. Now and again someone from the medical staff would come forward, but with nothing new to say. Johnny spent a lot of time crying into his hands, and I brought him drinks from a vending machine I'd found while we waited.

"In the end, Dave phoned his story through to the *Echo* as it stood. This is it, hot off the press." He opened out the rolled-up newspaper to reveal a minor front-page item lacking photographs. "You won't find anything in it you don't already know. It must've been five thirty, probably later, before we heard anything. I called Sophie, and she said she'd drive down for me. Most of the reporters had gone, but I'd waited because I'd sensed all along there was something badly wrong. It was because of what someone had said earlier at the harbor—that when they'd fished her out of the water, she'd looked as though she'd been in it for days. I hadn't been able to get that out of my head.

"I was back at the vending machine when I noticed some of the surgeons and police muttering together along the hall outside pathology. One of the police came forward, asking whether any of us were related to the girl, or who could identify her, and Johnny stood up.

"He seemed to be gone forever. By the time he came out, Sophie had arrived, worried and more then a little pissed off with me for not calling sooner."

Sophie tried to force a smile, leaning forward toward him to squeeze his hand. "It was awful, when Johnny came out," she said. "The first thing we heard were these sounds, these great round howls that made me think of wild animals. It took me a second to realize it was Johnny screaming. Then the howls became easier to recognize, and he was shouting and babbling—not that you could make sense of the words —and then he was coming toward us with two nurses holding him up and the others, the police and one of the surgeons, watching."

"At first we didn't dare ask what was wrong," Darren said. "You could see it was more than grief: the look on his face was something I'd never seen before."

"Like yours when I opened the door just now," Leigh said. "And you hadn't seen what Johnny Cross had."

"Not that I'd want to," Sophie said. "We decided to take him away from there as fast as we could, get him home if he couldn't or didn't want to drive. In fact, it turned out he wanted company, wanted someone to talk to, so we looked for a café that was open. He was still blubbering when we got inside, with the staff and customers giving us looks. You'd think they didn't know how it feels to be upset.

"I started by asking Johnny if he wanted to talk about what he'd seen, and although he said yes, he took his time getting around to it. He kept breaking down and saying how much he'd loved her, and how beautiful Isabelle was, or used to be." Stopping herself short, Sophie nudged Darren. "You'd better finish, I don't think I can."

Good God, Leigh thought, I'm not sure I want to hear this. Haven't they been doing what Johnny did ever since they came here, avoiding the worst, deferring the moment until they can't put it off any longer?

Outside, something flurried through the branches of one of the blackened, shifting trees. Opposite Leigh, Joan sat rigid and intense, cracking the knuckles of one hand in the palm of the other.

"When they let him into the room," Darren said, "she was lying there under a sheet with the lights down, all except for a spot directly above the body. The pathologist gave some sort of speech at that point. This isn't going to be easy or pleasant, he said; do try to be prepared for a shock. And one of the cops—I think he said it was one of the cops—was standing by the trolley they had her on and was saying, Would you please take your time and tell us if this is her.

"Then, as Johnny walked toward her, the pathologist said quickly: Don't touch her; whatever you do, don't touch her. By that time the policeman had already lifted the sheet. And Johnny lost control.

"From what we could gather, she was still recognizable, but only just. Her eyes were closed, her hair was long and dark the way he remembered it, but the rest . . ."

"Don't stop," Joan said sharply. "You're going to have to say it eventually; you may as well get it over with now."

Darren swallowed drily before going on. His eyes were no longer focused, at least not on anything in the room. "He said there were no marks he could see on her, but he knew right away she couldn't have drowned, or if she had, there was more to it than that. Her skin was so pale it was—what did he call it?"

"Translucent," Sophie said flatly.

"But worse, the life had been sucked out of her, every good thing, every glimmer. Whatever happened to Isabelle had *changed* her."

"Changed her?" Leigh almost choked. "Changed her how?"

"Made her old."

It was, Leigh thought, the one word she'd least expected to hear. Almost anything else would have surprised her less. She'd feared drowning, asphyxiation, mutilation, all of the many bad ways to go, but she hadn't bargained for this.

"How . . . ?" she began, fumbling, not knowing what to ask or how to ask it. "Old? What exactly do you mean?"

"Old," Darren said, "as in old, or older. Her skin was baggy, with lines where she hadn't had any before. And you have to understand I'm describing this second-hand, Johnny was in tears when he told us this. I don't believe he was saying she looked like an old person, but that she'd suddenly become worn out, exhausted—"

"Spent," Sophie added conclusively. "Seeing her like that sent him crazy for a second, and he grabbed at her hand. That was when all hell broke loose. The pathologist screaming, the cop running around to drag Johnny away, Johnny beginning to throw his fit—those were the screams we heard first."

"But Jesus, no wonder," Joan said, shaking her head, now cracking the knuckles on her other hand, one by one. "No wonder he started screaming. Who wouldn't, seeing something like that? That's horrible; just utterly horrible."

"It wasn't only what he saw," Darren said. "That was bad enough, but it wasn't what tipped him over the edge. He started screaming when Isabelle's hand came away in his."

I knew it, Leigh thought. I knew I was not going to want to hear this.

She could only feel grateful to be sitting. If she tried to rise now, she wouldn't be able, since her limbs were suddenly numb as her mind. Somewhere inside her, she sensed the weight come down again, the weight that had briefly lifted itself this evening when Joan had returned the envelope from Apollo Introductions. If the morning at Tech had left an impression of gas seeping in through a convenient keyhole, then this was a fog, a seamless white fog passing into her room through the open window.

"But what *happened* to her?" Joan wondered, suddenly scraping her chair back, standing abruptly, pacing the room, unable to settle herself a moment longer. "Has anyone the faintest idea what caused such a change? And so suddenly, overnight?"

"That's what the authorities will be asking themselves," Sophie said. "Chances are, if they had an explanation, they would have had *something* to tell the press, if only to stop the speculation. This, though, isn't your everyday situation. It's more like something out of some sci-fi film. If you want to know what I really think, I don't know *what* to think. I'm terrified."

Me too, Leigh thought, me too. "And Johnny Cross?"

"Tonight he managed to drive home alone," Sophie said. "He's sharing an apartment with friends in Westbourne, so at least he'll have company. We got his address, and we thought we'd head over there tomorrow. Chances are he'll need more than the kind of help we can give, though."

"I wouldn't be surprised," Joan murmured, hugging herself for dear life. "God, just the thought's enough to send you over. Oh, I feel sick. This is just too horrible. Too horrible for words."

• • •

By the time the others had made their excuses and left—Darren and Sophie for an early night; Joan to meet Graham —it was almost ten. The last hour had been one long uneasy silence broken by failed attempts to talk of other, lighter things. They had sipped tea and shaken their heads helplessly while the shadow of Isabelle Brooks closed over the room.

At least they're leaving it behind them, Leigh thought weakly when they'd gone. But the shadow's still here, a very large darkness in a very small room. And now I'm alone with it. She turned on the TV that was mounted on one wall to save floor space and fell into bed.

Like everything else that night, the lead reports on *News at Ten* washed over her without leaving any lasting impression. The only picture that meant anything as she drifted toward sleep was the one behind her eyes, the one she would have given anything to be rid of: the image of Isabelle's hand crumbling to nothing as Johnny took hold of it, like a prize made of clay.

· 5 ·

Several times in the night Leigh awoke sharply, overheated and sweating, even though she'd kicked off the covers. As she lay on her back and stared up toward the ceiling she couldn't see, sounds drifted in and out: trees bristled beyond her window; soft, near weightless footsteps passed along the hall, pausing outside her door before moving on. A little later, voices boomed argumentatively elsewhere in the building, voices she thought she knew but didn't have the energy to place.

By the time she dragged herself out of bed, hours earlier than usual, her dreams had faded almost completely. There was only the lingering memory of a vast, bottomless darkness unfolding before her, of here and there glimmers of light like fading stars, and the constant sound of waves caressing the shore.

It was barely six thirty, but she couldn't lie there doing nothing. Collecting her towels and toiletry bag, she unlocked her door and crossed to her private bathroom opposite.

Each of the apartments in Silverwood Dene had its own; no doubt hers was the only one larger than the room it belonged to.

For a full five minutes she managed to forget herself under the shower. Her mind needed cleansing as well as her body. As she turned off the flow, seized the nearest towel and began drying herself, she heard something thump in the hall, not far away; footsteps again, or a door. It was probably hers, which she habitually left unlocked whenever she used the bathroom. Her open window must have created a through draft, opening and slamming the door. Even so, she thought she sensed movement along the hall to her right as she left the bathroom, clutching her damp belongings.

Leigh turned to look. There was no one there, though she couldn't help feeling that someone had flitted out of sight only seconds before she'd glanced that way. They could have ducked toward the stairs or into one of the other rooms. Still, the poor light—only two of the four bare lightbulbs were working—didn't inspire her to investigate.

She'd jumped inside her room and swung the door shut, dropping the latch, before she remembered what had made her so jumpy. For a while, before the shower had brought her to, the news of Isabelle had seemed like a dream.

Being up and about before first light didn't help her feel any less disoriented. She sat at the table, munching granola without appetite, poring over the local paper Darren had left. The electric light made her shadow fall across the print. The front-page story about Isabelle contained nothing new, didn't even mention her by name. Turning five or six pages in rapid succession, Leigh found herself at the small ads. It was the column headed Personal that drew her eye.

In it, among inserts for kissograms, help lines and typing services, were several for local and national dating agencies. Some, like Apollo, preferred the term *introductions*; others were less stuffy about the services they offered. Apollo's was the last name in the column, before Articles Wanted began.

Leigh closed the paper with a snap and looked away, trying to clear her head of what she was thinking. The first thing she saw as she did was the envelope. Finishing her granola, she never lifted her eyes from it, hardly even felt herself blink. Long before she'd finished school or left home for college, she'd regularly scanned the personal columns and fantasized about whom she might meet, how it might turn out; yet she'd never done more then fantasize. She hadn't needed to, was why. She would meet the right man in her own time. No need to force it.

Then why was she so close to forcing it now? Why was she pushing aside her empty dish to reach for the crumpled envelope, unfolding the sheets she'd thrown away yesterday while hoping against hope they'd find their way back to her?

Because it was meant to be, she thought with some certainty, with a clarity that felt like the sun coming up. Because *it* found *you*, not the other way around. Not once, but twice, because Joan brought it back when she couldn't have known you wanted her to. It *was* meant to be. It's as simple as that.

For the next ten or twelve minutes she was in a trance. Her every action felt programmed as she searched out a pen, filled in the questionnaire without hesitation, then sat to re-read the covering letter. *No money, no obligation,* it boasted at one point. At another, *Your chance to meet someone just like yourself—someone who values the friendship of others above all else.* Below this were lists of activities—parties, informal gatherings, vacations, country walks—that the agency encouraged its members to join in. Leigh closed her eyes for a minute, trying to imagine the kinds of people this might attract. Would there be others like her? Lonely, normal people; people with needs they couldn't take to their friends and relatives? Surely they wouldn't all be too old, or ugly, or dull, all of love's outcasts bandying together?

Your chance to meet someone just like yourself, she thought, and opened her eyes again.

• • •

She gave herself no time for second thoughts. There was a mailbox around the corner on Dean Park Road, not far from the cricket ground, and it wasn't until she'd seen her envelope disappear into it that she began to wonder.

Leigh stood contemplating the black rectangle that had swallowed her reply. Had she been too impulsive, rushing into her clothes, hurrying from the apartment with letter in hand? Couldn't it have waited until she'd regained her senses? After all, yesterday's horror story would have made anyone lose control, do things they wouldn't normally dream of. She'd thrown herself into the questionnaire without a thought, as if that would help her forget everything else.

But unless she waited two hours or so for the first pick-up, missing her lift to college, there was nothing she could do. Even then, there'd be no guarantee that a mail carrier emptying the box would allow her to keep the letter. The thing was sent off, and that was that.

She strolled along Cavendish, slowing as she neared the stumpy white gateposts outside Silverwood Dene. In the time it had taken her to dash out with her letter, the sun had risen, warming her face and hands, and the day had begun. O'Reilly, the landlord, carried two swollen garbage bags from the building to the communal dumpster in the forecourt as she came up the drive. Seeing Leigh approaching, he at once slowed and straightened himself, throwing out his chest, swinging the hefty bags he was carrying as if they were nothing. Was that meant to impress her?

Nothing else about him did. He was wearing a pair of tattered jeans and a vest that was stained as if he'd tipped his breakfast down it. He was tall and fit, with well-toned muscles, but there was a steeliness in his gaze, a darkness, that made her wary. Even as she fumbled out her key ring and made for the front door, she felt him staring, mentally undressing her. By the time she reached the door, she was trying so hard not to stare back, she was shaking. Please ignore me, she thought. Please forget you ever saw me.

"Good morning," he said then, and her heart sank. "Up and about at the crack of dawn today, eh?"

"Mmmm," she managed.

"Busy day ahead, perhaps."

"Mmmm, yes."

She heard the two separate thuds of his bags going into the dumpster and began to panic. This is mad, she told herself sternly; he's only making conversation and look at you! Her fingers were trembling, the six or seven keys on her ring were suddenly impossibly alike. And now she sensed—she didn't need to look up to know—that O'Reilly was walking toward her.

"Having trouble? Anything I can do to help?"

"No!" she almost shouted, barely keeping herself in check.

Then, more calmly, "No, everything's fine, really." She raised one key to the lock, but that proved to be the one for her locker at college.

"Wait, I have the master key here somewhere." O'Reilly was stuffing a hand into his pocket. "I'll save you the trouble."

Before he could go any further, she'd found what she wanted. The front door key was fractionally smaller and more polished than the rest, and she ought to have found it easily. Doing her best to make her rush seem like cool efficiency, she twisted it in the lock, stepped neatly inside, began closing the door.

Through the gap she saw a lopsided smile fade on O'Reilly's lips as he searched his jeans pockets. He began to speak, but the door was already cutting him off.

"Thanks anyway," Leigh said.

"Don't mention it."

As soon as she heard him go, she relaxed, but trudging up to her room, she imagined how foolish she must have seemed, and felt herself flush. Perhaps there was something wrong with her: she was starting to see the worst in everything and everyone these days. Was this what living in a box —in a coffin—did to you if you lived in one long enough? Couldn't even O'Reilly have redeeming features? After all, it was only his look and his manner that worried her; he'd never actually done anything to make her dislike him.

• • •

College came and went almost unnoticed that day, relief of a kind. At least she hadn't had to face the model in the life class again; she doubted she would have been able to cope with that. Instead, locked away in the paint workshop, she primed several new canvases and set to work on an abstract she'd started some weeks before.

It was something she was painting in grays, whites and metallic blues, and the thrill of it was that it allowed her to work with wild, flowing brush strokes and thick dabs of paint, forgetting for long hours who she was and what she was trying to hide from. Perhaps she needed to work on it for many weeks yet before she knew what it was, but right now the painting was therapy. The churning grays and blues transported her.

The drawback was that she worked through lunch and had to take coffee breaks at irregular times. She didn't see anyone all day. Sophie should have been in 3-D building a papier-mâché man, though there was no sign of her when Leigh poked her head around the door. Joan and Darren were probably out on location with their cameras. Or perhaps they'd all headed down to see Johnny Cross.

No one came to her room that evening. Joan never called, though the unmistakable thump-thump of rhythmic music rose from Joan's room later on. At some point there was a scream, and the sound of glass breaking, and laughter. She must be with Graham, Leigh decided.

And wherever Darren and Sophie are, they'll be together as well.

Everyone is with someone. And look at me. Just look at me.

In her box-room that felt more than ever like the coffin Sophie had likened it to, she lay on her bed with the TV on but the sound turned down and waited. Waited for the onset of sleep, and for the noises downstairs to subside. Most of all she waited for the phone to ring or the mail to bring a message that might change everything forever.

As it happened, she only had to wait until morning.

• • •

She hardly dared look at the mail she gathered up from the stand after breakfast. Again it was early, thirty or forty minutes before Sophie was due, and, ridiculously, her heart was racing.

There were three items in all. The first was a postcard from her father, who apparently was vacationing in Greece with the woman he'd left home for. There was an official window envelope containing a statement from the bank. And lastly, something from Apollo Introductions, addressed in that now-familiar hand, which had somehow arrived without a stamp. She tore open the envelope as she headed upstairs and was reading it before she reached her room.

Dear Leigh, it read. Her name was handwritten, the rest printed. *Thank you for contacting Apollo. Let us assure you, you have chosen wisely! Opportunities to improve your life seldom arise, but this is one of them!* Whoever had composed this certainly had a fondness for exclamation marks. *Whether you are looking for love or hoping to meet people and establish new friendships, Apollo is here to help you!*

Much of what followed read like run-of-the-mill junk mail: You *shall* go to the ball, you *will* win the prize draw, and so on and so forth. Here and there she skipped lines. Nevertheless, the final paragraph intrigued her enough to read it twice:

To reiterate, then, we are NOT like other agencies we could mention. We do NOT use computer techniques since we hold the belief that people are not to be treated as numbers. And when we say there is no obligation on your part, that's exactly what we mean! Those exclamations were beginning to make her feel shouted at, but now she was approaching the punchline. *Therefore, without any obligation on your part, Apollo Introductions would like to invite you to a preliminary meeting—a party at which you can meet both members and prospective members like yourself. This is to take place at . . .*

What followed was an address on Sea Road in Boscombe, again handwritten, and a date. It took her a second to realize how near the date was: the party was set for tomorrow night.

Leigh sat on her bed and tried to think. Not that her life was so packed she first had to check her diary; but suppose she felt out of place there? What if she ended the evening alone again? But good God, she thought, looking around her. What's this if not out of place? What's this if not alone?

In her haste to read the letter, she'd overlooked something else in the envelope, which she now shook onto her palm to examine. It was a tiny ceramic bird captured in flight and mounted on a stud. The bird was a canary, she decided, a caged bird set free. It was meant to be worn as a lapel pin or tie tack—perhaps all members were expected to wear one, signifying they belonged. Well, whether she attended or not, she wasn't committed to anything yet. She tossed the thing onto her bedside table and started to dress for college.

There was no answer from Joan's room when she knocked almost half an hour later. Outside, the Citroën's horn sounded three times. She knocked again, but there was still no reply, not even a grunt. "Knew it'd catch up with you in the end," she told Joan's door, and set off.

"Well, her curtains are closed," Sophie observed as Leigh shuffled in and along the backseat. "Do you think we should give her a minute?"

"Let her sleep it off," Darren said. "By the looks of her yesterday, she needs it." Sophie nodded and began to reverse out. "Course you didn't see her yesterday, did you Leigh? No one saw *you*. Where were you?"

"Oh, just painting. What do you mean about Joan?"

"Just that she looked so wasted, all dark patches around the eyes and her eyes all bloodshot and her face so pale. Whatever she's into, she's definitely overdoing it."

"All I know is it sounds like fun," Leigh said, bracing herself as Sophie cornered. "The parties in her room, I mean."

"That Graham's to blame," Sophie said. "She makes him sound like a dream—the very thing she's been looking for. And you know, she really *does* sound in love, and seriously. But take one look at the state of her and how can you say he's doing her any good?"

Leigh flinched as Darren turned on the in-car hi-fi and Public Enemy began jabbering behind her. After a moment he lowered the volume.

"Did you get down to see Johnny Cross?" she asked.

Darren waited until Sophie had pulled onto Lansdowne Road, then twisted to face Leigh. "We arrived, but there wasn't much point in staying. He'd been on a drinking binge ever since Monday, and the place reeked to high heaven. A friend of his, a student from Malta, was brewing black coffee all the while we were there and trying to calm Johnny down. Johnny was fairly much out of his skull. He kept going on about murder, and swearing revenge. Against who, though?" Darren gave an emphatic shrug. "How can anyone call what happened to Isabelle murder? It's unique, right enough, but even the surgeons aren't calling it murder."

"I'm beginning to wonder, though," Sophie said, "how much of what Johnny says we can take at face value."

Darren half turned toward her. "Meaning what?"

"I saw the mess he was in for myself. He was much the same when we met at the hospital on Monday. Seems to me he's basically unstable. And no one else saw what happened in the pathology lab, did they? Only Johnny."

"The surgeon did," Leigh said. "And the policeman who was there."

"But they didn't talk about what happened," Sophie went on. "All we know is that Johnny came out screaming and shouting, held on his feet by two nurses, and told us some horror story, but as yet we haven't confirmed anything he said. We've assumed an awful lot. We were shell-shocked because of Isabelle, and we swallowed the rest whole."

Darren was shaking his head, though. "But there was something *different* about him when he came out. He was grieving before that, certainly, but keeping himself together all the same. He *did* see something in there, I'm sure."

"Maybe he just saw Isabelle." Sophie paid scant attention to the oncoming vehicles sounding their horns as she overtook a slow-moving van, crossing the white line in the process. "Wouldn't that have been enough to make him lose control?"

"Then why would he make up the rest?" Leigh wondered.

"Because he didn't know he was inventing. He actually believed it had happened. Emotionally he was so hyped up, he imagined it all, every last detail. That's all I'm suggesting: Johnny's still disoriented and in shock, and perhaps it's wrong to take anything he's saying on faith at the moment."

Darren was skeptical. "All the same, Johnny Cross was as stable as you or I when I first ran into him at the harbor yesterday, and somewhere between then and now he became unhinged. And daft as it sounds, I still believe that what he saw in that room unhinged him."

It was all conjecture, of course. No one really knew anything. And perhaps because of the shock waves Isabelle's death had sent through the Tech, there had been too much loose talk and wild speculation already. Sophie was making good sense; after all, weren't the wildest, least probable stories the ones you most wanted to believe?

But by the time they turned in at the college parking lot, Leigh had realized with a shock that, like Darren, she believed the worst anyway.

· 6 ·

Then again, her feelings about everything were fluctuating lately. It was nearing that time of the month again. Most often she sailed through her periods with hardly a tremor or twinge, but occasionally the pain would be acute, the world would rush at her screaming and she'd feel close to losing control, as now. This, she imagined, was not going to be one of those months she sailed through.

No wonder she felt like a cat on hot bricks, unable to sleep or relax. It was laughable, the way she'd allowed the mail solicitation to dominate her. Ordinarily she wouldn't let such a trivial thing become such an issue. What she needed was a change—perhaps the kind of change the party would bring. And at the first opportunity she was going to request —no, *demand*—a better room at the Dene. Either that or she'd be out. O'Reilly could go to hell. She wouldn't tolerate the Coffin any longer, not now she knew what it was doing to her.

Again, standing before her canvas, working the paint back

and forth, seemed to free her, to lighten her. She was part of the painting now, though it took her until afternoon break to see what it represented. Suddenly thirsty, she put down her brushes and stepped back, unlocking herself from the swirling colors.

It was the sea, she knew at once. She was painting a storm, which was odd, since nothing of the sort had crossed her mind while she'd worked on it. The deep grays and metallic blues were waves, the flecks of white crests of foam. Was this her subconscious at work or what? Could you paint such things without knowing?

Tim Wright, her group tutor, had always been one for sneering at abstracts, at least those from students who hadn't mastered representational work. Painting abstracts too soon, he'd once told her, was like running before you could walk. Do me a bowl of fruit or flowers first; *then* do your abstract.

Well, he wouldn't sneer now, Leigh thought as she left for break. She hadn't been painting an abstract after all.

• • •

There was no reply from Joan when she got back, even though she'd noticed from outside that Joan's curtains were still drawn. She waited a minute or two after knocking, even putting her ear to the door, but there was no sound within. Maybe Joan had eloped with Graham. If not, she'd simply gone away without leaving a message.

She'd intended to tell Joan about the invitation. Perhaps it was wiser not to anyway, since the evening could still prove to be a flop not worth mentioning. In which case she'd only feel foolish for having gone.

As she puttered barefoot about, preparing supper, she felt her stomach slowly tighten, her heartbeat speed up. This time her nervous tension wasn't only premenstrual: it was as if her body were ticking off minutes to tomorrow night's party.

• • •

She could have saved herself the worry. The gathering in Boscombe was everything she'd hoped it wouldn't be.

Arriving soon after eight, she twice passed the house on Sea Road where the lights and soft music were before plucking up the courage to go in. Even then, reaching the front door, she had a vision of herself ringing the bell and running away like a child playing trick-or-treat. She knew she'd made a mistake when she saw the thirtyish woman answering the door in a halter-neck black evening dress and pearl necklace.

The woman seemed to falter at first. Blocking the doorway, a near-empty champagne flute in one hand, she studied Leigh slowly and critically. Finally a smile found her lips, though not the rest of her face. There was a sadness about her, Leigh realized then, as strong as cheap perfume.

"Are you one of us?" the woman said. "I'm sorry, that is, are you here for the bash?"

It was Leigh who faltered now, and at first she almost cried out, No, I must have the wrong address, I'm supposed to be visiting friends. But instead she said, "I suppose so, yes."

"Then come in, dear," the woman said, stepping aside. "I'm Maggie. Pleased to meet you."

• • •

It took Leigh less than a minute to confirm what she'd known as soon as the front door opened. The party was like an accident. All human life was here, and she couldn't relate to any of it.

In one corner, dignified, formally dressed men and women kept themselves to themselves. In another, several fortyish men clutching Guinness bottles and smoking roll-your-owns stared silently toward a group of women in cheap furs and fishnet tights. Sprawled at the foot of the stairs, two aging punkettes gazed into space. Wherever you looked there were cliques. Some might have belonged to the five-star restaurant circuit, others to pubs and nightclubs, still others to park benches and flophouses. None was trying to cross over. It was like twenty separate parties colliding, Leigh thought, her head still spinning.

Even the music fazed her. One minute Morrissey, the next Count Basie. There were different soundtracks in different rooms. Good God, could she ever admit to Joan she'd been here? She'd never live it down if she did. She was heading for the door she'd entered by when a man carrying two tall tumblers stumbled into her path.

Her immediate reaction was to smile timidly and sidestep, but as she did, he came with her, again blocking the way.

"Drink?" he said, pushing one of the tumblers toward her, and for the first time she found his face.

He must have been twice her age. Not only that, but his eyes were glazed, presumably from drink, and his thinning hair was pinned back with so much Brylcreem, his scalp shone. He had on a well-fitted, double-breasted suit, and on one lapel he was wearing his ceramic bird pin with pride. In fact he thrust his chest toward her as he said, "You're awfully young to be attending one of these bashes, aren't you?"

"You're as young as you feel," Leigh said, and thought, What on earth are you *talking* about?

Again he pushed the tumbler toward her, nudging her hand with it until she had no choice but to take it.

His face clouded over. He leaned nearer as if unable to balance, and for an instant she feared he would fall. Then his head jerked back and he smiled broadly with perfectly white capped teeth. "You know, I noticed you the minute you walked in. Said to myself, you've got to talk to that lady. She's exactly what this flagging party needs."

"Me?" Leigh said incredulously. The front door loomed just beyond the man's left shoulder. "You must be confusing me with someone else."

"Really, you shouldn't run yourself down like that."

"But I wasn't—"

"The problem," the man continued, "is that living alone gives us too much time to think. We become so that we only see the bad in ourselves. Don't you agree? If no one loves us, we're bound to feel, in the end, it's because something's wrong with us, we're not worth loving. What I mean is that . . . What I mean is . . . " He seemed to be losing his thread. He lowered his gaze, frowned, then seemed to find what he'd lost.

"You're single, of course," he asserted. "Then again, aren't we all? Ha ha. I wasn't, you know, until last August. My wife up and left me, took both of the children. Jenny, who's ten, Malcolm, who's seven. One fine sunny morning. Left me high and dry without so much as a note, just a phone call after she'd driven two hundred miles. . . .

"And then my business went under."

Not only was he waffling, he was now close to tears as well. Oh help, Leigh thought; I didn't come here for this—I really don't need this now. It would have been easier to feel sympathy for the sad sack if he hadn't come begging for it, blocking her path to the door in the process. But he wasn't making it easy for himself. His Brylcreem was suffocating; the drink he'd brought was raw as unsweetened lemon at the back of her throat. And now his face was reddening, his whole body stooping forward as if at any minute he was going to grab hold of her. There were probably hundreds of men like him out here, so desperate for company they were driving away almost everyone they met.

All at once she had to be out of this place. "I'm sorry," she said, returning her tumbler to his hand as she stepped toward the gap that had opened between his right shoulder and the wall. "I'm sorry, but I really shouldn't have come here. I don't know what I was looking for, but I expected—"

"You can't be leaving, not so soon."

"I think so, yes. I have to."

"It's me you're running from, isn't it? I'm opening my heart to you and you don't want to know."

"It isn't like that," she pleaded. "It has to do with what *I'm* looking for; it's not you, believe me."

"Bitch," he said. "You're just like the rest."

It was spoken with such venom, she felt she'd been punched. Had he really said that? At first she doubted her hearing. Well, she wouldn't allow the remark to throw her, otherwise the scene might turn ugly. So much for meeting people like herself. Staring fixedly ahead, she eased past him and started toward the door, where a dark-haired young man she'd never seen before stood waiting, fingering the latch, his face gradually brightening as she approached. Even before he spoke, in the instant their eyes met, she felt a flush of embarrassment mingling with pleasure. He was casually dressed in a black track-suit top and tan cord jeans. His eyes were deep brown, his smile generous.

"It's all right," he said quietly. "He's not following you. Looks like he's in search of another victim."

She laughed—more from nervous politeness than amusement—and turned to see the man carrying both full tumblers toward the kitchen.

"Leaving already?" the young man asked, easing the door open slightly.

"Well, yes. This isn't what I expected."

"Me neither." She just had time to register the pin he was wearing before he added, "Well, they *did* say no obligation. That means no one's obligated to stay."

Before she knew what was happening, he had stepped outdoors with her, matching her step as she walked down the drive to the road. At the gate, they paused, facing one another uncertainly. A cool night breeze cut up the rising street, bringing the smell and the sound of waves from the bay.

"Well," he said.

"Well," she replied, and swallowed drily.

"Good night, then."

"Yes. Good night."

Nevertheless, they set off in the same direction, toward the main street. They even walked shoulder to shoulder. After twenty or thirty paces, Leigh glanced toward him in just the same instant he glanced at her. They broke into laughter at once.

"You're not so easy to get rid of," she said.

"Who, me? Just say the word and I'll vanish," he said then, slowing as they reached the junction on Hawkwood Road. "As a matter of fact, I was going to say something like The night is still young! But that sounds so awful, doesn't it?"

Leigh shook her head slowly, emphatically. "Not at all. Not to me, anyway." Suddenly she wanted to laugh again. She no longer felt nerve racked; she was wholly at ease. "Was that your way of asking me something?"

"It could have been," he replied. "All I was going to mention was that I'm parked around the corner near Sainsburys. And if you'd like a lift home, or anywhere else . . ."

He didn't need to say more.

• • •

Twenty minutes later they were facing one another across a table in a pizzeria in Bournemouth center. Stephen—full name Stephen Roth, she'd learned—was pouring out house red from a half-liter carafe while Leigh toyed with her side salad. Although they'd hardly stopped talking since walking out onto Sea Road, she was grateful for the lull, which gave her a chance to remind herself this *was* really happening, it *wasn't* a flight of fancy. When he finished pouring and looked up, a pleasurable shiver ran through her.

"You know," he said, "you really don't strike me as the sort who'd need to go through an agency. You're outgoing and easy enough to talk to. It isn't as though you'd have trouble meeting others."

"Let's say I *thought* I had problems that way. And if I hadn't been there tonight, I'd probably still feel that. I'd still be wondering what I was missing." She waited until he'd handed her her glass, took a sip, and went on. "There are people out there who *are* in a bad way and need all the help they can get. Maybe I'm not one of them after all."

"You were lonely though," he said. "You don't have to be an extreme case to feel that."

"Yes. But I do have friends. That's more than can be said for some."

"And sometimes being with friends can make you feel worse, wouldn't you say?"

She considered for a minute. She thought of Darren with Sophie, Joan with Graham. Yes, she had friends, but in a sense was still an outsider. "What about you, though? I can't see why you would've been drawn to Apollo. For one thing, you're so easy to get along with, and for another, you look so—" She put a hand to her mouth before she got carried away, then found herself stifling a laugh. "Sorry. Didn't mean to embarrass you."

"That's all right. I can take all the embarrassment you want to dish out. Keep going." Collecting his knife and fork, he began sawing into his chili beef pizza slice. "If you really want to know, I need a change."

"From what?"

"Bad feelings, I suppose. A relationship that didn't work out."

"You don't have to tell me if you don't want," Leigh said, suddenly anxious not to change the mood for the worse.

Stephen made a nonchalant gesture, as if swatting a fly. "That's all right. I would've told you sooner or later anyway. As a matter of fact, there've been several that broke down, even though some were quite—well, very involved. God knows why these things keep happening. Someone always ends up being hurt. I've just had a bad run, I suppose."

"Well, you shouldn't have," Leigh said. "You deserve better than that." And then stopped herself. After all, they had met only thirty minutes ago, and here she was practically throwing herself at him.

Hold on, she told herself sternly, spearing a tomato slice with her fork. There's no need to rush; what will be will be. Otherwise you're like the Brylcreem man, frightening everyone away, so anxious for success you're doomed to failure.

She managed to take just enough time over her pizza slice and her next mouthful of wine that the moment had passed when she spoke again.

"I notice you're wearing one of those things," she said, indicating his tie tack.

"Oh, this? I thought everyone would be."

"I decided not to. Until I knew what was involved."

"And now you know." Laying down his fork, he removed the pin and dropped it into the ashtray. Then he fixed her again with those dark eyes in which she was slowly losing herself. In fact, for a second she was lost entirely, until she sensed him feeling for her hand across the table, interlacing his fingers with hers.

"Are we hitting it off as well as I think?" he said.

"I hope so. I really do."

"Can we do this again?"

"Just say the word."

• • •

He drove her home early, before the pubs closed and the roads filled with drunken drivers. As Stephen slowed, nearing the entrance to Silverwood Dene, Leigh very nearly invited him in. Instead, she took a deep breath and said nothing. Another night, perhaps. Another night, definitely. But now she needed time to savor the evening, to run through it all again as she headed toward sleep; not spoil the opportunity by rushing or forcing.

Incredibly, he seemed to understand even this. For a time they sat in the car in the dark, the engine still running, her heart beating so loudly, she was sure he would hear it. Yet it wasn't anxiety this time; if anything the steady rhythm soothed her.

His hand, a silhouette, reached for her face and she turned gratefully into it. Then he leaned closer, kissing her lightly on the mouth before backing away.

"Tomorrow, did we say?" he wondered.

"We didn't say, but yes, I'd love to."

"Then I'll pick you up from here. About seven?"

"You're on."

• • •

The first thing that passed through her mind when she woke the next morning set the pattern for her day. She hadn't been dreaming. She had met someone new and exciting—not only that, but someone as enchanted by her as she was by him.

The spell Stephen Roth had cast over her seemed to strengthen, not fade, as the morning progressed, as she showered and dressed and breakfasted with an appetite she hadn't had for weeks. Again there was no response from Joan when she went downstairs to check at eight thirty. Joan *had* eloped with Graham, then.

No matter; she knew in her own mind how right this was —she didn't need anyone to tell her. If the brightness she sensed in herself told her anything, it was that she couldn't be wrong. She didn't even let slip to Sophie when she called her to announce that she wouldn't be in college today.

Shouldn't she be racked with guilt, heading downtown to the shops while others were slaving away at the Tech? Not that she knew of anyone who *slaved* there. She browsed at the perfume counter in Beales, bought a pair of khaki cord trousers and a white cable sweater at Marks, then indulged in coffee and doughnuts at the tearoom just off the square.

Later, lost among paperback novels in Smith's, she wondered when she'd last been so impulsive, merely taken a day and done with it as she'd pleased. She couldn't remember. Not once this term, not even on weekends. Suddenly she felt such a swell of relief, she hardly knew what to do with it. If only Stephen were here, browsing alongside her! Wouldn't that make the morning complete? On impulse, she bought two novels by Mary Wesley and one by Sue Townsend with money she couldn't afford to burn.

Everything after that was killing time before Stephen came to collect her. When she heard his car in the forecourt, she jumped, seized her banana-shaped bag and ran.

Outside, the air held a promise of spring becoming summer, a mild warmth that made her feel she was slowly waking, coming alive. When she glanced back at the Dene, she saw O'Reilly peering through his lace-curtained window. She couldn't and didn't want to read his expression. It was tempting to make a show of being with someone—that would tell O'Reilly where to get off—but as soon as she saw Stephen beaming behind the wheel, and the spray of yellow miniature roses on the backseat, she wanted only to be herself.

It was his idea to take in a film, even though two hours in the dark, half-empty theater seemed such a waste when she thought of the weather outside. Not that it mattered; she was content to be with Stephen again, more than content, almost edgy. Though the film was a Mel Gibson thriller she'd normally have relished, tonight she had to force herself to concentrate. Knowing Stephen was beside her diverted her attention. When she sensed him turning to glance at her, or felt the touch of his hand on hers, whole sections of the film went begging. Dialogue scenes, pieces of plot, jokes that sent the rest of the audience into fits passed her by altogether. Much of what happened between the explosions and gunshots made no sense at all. In the end she was relieved when the credits rolled and the screen filled with silhouetted heads in a hurry to leave.

Outside, Westover Road was a carnival. Couples were clambering into and out of cars, and lines formed at the ice rink and outside the theater for the late show. The impression she had was of bright lights, high spirits, strong primal colors. Passing among the crowds, arm in arm with Stephen, she thought, I'm part of this, too. *We're* part of it, aren't we?

At a bar in the International Center they sat drinking mulled wine at a table overlooking the Pleasure Gardens through large, smoked-glass windows. Stephen was twenty-two and had worked at a Superprint shop on Old Christchurch Road since dropping out of college three years ago.

"And your family?" Leigh wanted to know. "Do they live far away?"

"A fair distance, yes. But we never got along. They were glad to see me go, and in the end I was happy to oblige them."

"That's terrible."

"Only if you look at it a certain way. My view is, it helped me find independence early. We had nothing in common; we're better off apart. It's history now."

"I still think it's sad." Not least because it was so close to home. After all, hadn't she also been ushered away to college within months of her parents' splitting up? Chances were she would have gone eventually, though not so hurriedly. "Don't you sometimes wish things could have been normal?" she asked.

"Who wants to be normal anyway?" After a beat, he relaxed in his chair, smiling easily. "Let's not spoil things by discussing me. You don't want to hear it. I'm the least interesting person I know."

"I can't second that," she said. "There's so much I still want to learn."

"You'll be disappointed."

"Let me be the judge."

"Leigh, you're off your head." For an instant his eyes flared with warmth, inviting her in. Then he seemed to lose sight of her, to be gazing inward instead. "Anyone who wants to know someone like me has to be off their head."

She didn't believe it for a second, though she couldn't help feeling that something in him had changed since last night. He was slower, more solemn, his moods shifting.

"Is it anything you can discuss with me?" she asked as they made ready to leave.

Stephen looked at her, nonplussed. "Is what?"

"Whatever it is that's bothering you."

Taking her hand, he guided her to the exit. "Oh, that's nothing. I was just thinking."

"About?"

"About us. How easy it is. Hoping it doesn't—"

"Go on," she urged.

"Hoping it doesn't turn out like the rest."

It took her a minute to recover from that. "Surely you're not writing us off already? Aren't you going to give us a chance?"

"Of course. It's just that I've managed to foul things up before, and I want to avoid making it happen again."

"But you're talking as if everything that went wrong before was your fault. Doesn't it take two to make a relationship happen?"

"Yes. But only one to make it *un*happen."

• • •

His words were still echoing dully through her head ten minutes later as he drove her home. It wasn't that anything had changed; only that he'd voiced a fear they both felt—that something so easy, so full of promise, could still come to nothing. Yet what was there to foil it? Only us, she thought. Only us.

Well, she wouldn't let it happen.

In a way, she was glad his fears were out in the open. There should be no secrets between lovers, if that's what they were becoming. Sooner or later she'd ask about the others he'd known, since it might help Stephen to talk about them. It would take time for him to adjust to her, and her to him. They'd take all the time they needed. Then, when she'd kept him to herself long enough, she'd introduce him to Sophie and Joan.

Stephen saw the lights on Cavendish Road before she did.

Leigh was drifting, the car's headlights going slowly out of focus, when he nudged her and said, "Is there a fire?"

She strained forward against the seat belt to see. A hundred yards ahead on the left, just visible above the hedgerows and treetops, a large pale building shimmered in a confusion of light. At first sight she decided it must be a fire. It was only nearer that the flickering seemed too regular to be flames. Nearer still, the building became Silverwood Dene.

The forecourt was aglow with emergency services vehicles, an ambulance and at least two police cars, and a badly parked Ford from the *Echo*. A number of uniformed people were rushing back and forth in the blaze of lights. Several distorted voices crackled like static on a police radio channel, though the words were unclear.

Stephen pulled up at the head of the drive, just inside the gate. While two ambulancemen flitted toward the building with a stretcher, he said, "Do you want me to come in?"

"No, better not. Whatever this is, it doesn't look good. For residents only, probably."

Before she could step from the car, he drew her toward him and held on, as if for dear life. Leigh closed her eyes for as long as it took and, returning the embrace, thought quite clearly, I've got you: you're mine.

"I'll miss you," he said finally, and Leigh replied awkwardly, "So will I."

She waved and blew kisses as he reversed from the drive and vanished at speed along Cavendish. Even his changeable moods couldn't shake her. He was enough to distract her from anything, even the activity here, the wide-open front door, the anguished expression on the face of one young policeman she saw as she entered.

"Do you live here?" he asked.

She showed her key. He nodded, satisfied, and she strode through the entrance hall. Several elderly ground-floor residents were at their open apartment doors. Some were in groups, muttering among themselves, hunching their shoulders. Others were being pestered by local reporters, while a lank-haired photographer fired off flashes at random. Leigh slipped past, unnoticed. One white-haired man she'd always thought of as the General watched her go as if she were to blame for disturbing him. As she mounted the stairs, she saw a pale-faced O'Reilly coming down, followed closely by one of the police. As they passed, she heard O'Reilly say gravely, "That's one of her friends."

He could only mean Leigh. It was then, nearing the upper floor, that she sensed how close to home this was. On the landing a handful of residents were being ushered back to their rooms by a policeman in uniform. The door to Joan's room was wide open. A plainclothes officer stood at the threshold; there were movements and voices inside.

Approaching, Leigh had the sensation of wading through a dream, limbs restrained by heavy water. It couldn't be that all this fuss was for Joan, not when—

Then she remembered stopping by this morning, and at least twice yesterday, and awaiting a reply that never came. She'd assumed that Joan was away. Yet hadn't she at some point expected to hear a response, sensed a presence behind the door?

From what she could gauge as she neared the doorway, Joan's room was a mess. Nothing unusual about that; Joan always lived as if her place had been recently ransacked. She told herself—wanted to believe with all her heart—that the police were investigating a break-in. But then she had seen the ambulance waiting; she had watched the men rush indoors with the stretcher. It couldn't be true that the body on the stretcher they were carrying out was Joan's.

"Jesus God!" someone inside the room exclaimed. "I never saw anything like this in my life."

"I did, more's the pity," another said.

Leigh felt barely able to stand, let alone react. It was as though a sharp knife had been brought down through her mind, severing her thoughts into equal, unmatchable halves. The cops, Joan's room, the figure draped with a sheet on a stretcher: all these were simple and obvious pieces she didn't seem able to fit together. She stood there, helplessly watching, aghast. Perhaps her mouth gaped open, her eyes widened, her arms fell slack at her sides, but she wouldn't have known. In one silent, unearthly instant she saw the stretcher pass by, a pale hand exposed beneath a corner of the sheet, a hand that looked blue and crumpled with age.

It couldn't be Joan's. How stupid she'd been to imagine that! Not even too many late nights of excess could have caused such a change. Seeing her staring, one of the ambulancemen tugged down the sheet before edging past. No, it couldn't be Joan; but if what she'd seen had been one of the older residents, why had they been in Joan's room?

That's one of her friends, O'Reilly had told the policeman though, just a minute ago on the stairs. And since it was Leigh he'd pointed out, whose friends had he meant, if not Joan's?

"Please, miss, please," the uniformed cop was telling her, having dispersed the other residents. "You shouldn't be here

—there's nothing you can do." He was handling this as gently as possible, almost apologetically. "If you live here, please go to your room."

She took two faltering steps back. "What's happening? I have a friend who lives here . . ."

Was it the word *lives* or the mere fact that she'd asked that made the plainclothesman turn to look at her? He was still at the threshold, leaning against the door frame. His hard dark gaze didn't hold her; she felt safer with the young man in uniform.

"That's Joan's room," she tried to explain. "We're friends. I live upstairs."

The plainclothesman said flatly, "The name we were given is Joan Bradley. Is that right?"

Leigh swallowed and nodded.

"You're a friend?"

"Yes, a friend. We're at college together, the Technical College on Wallisdown. I know her as well as anyone here. I mean, if you need me to take a look at her . . ." She stopped herself there, or was stopped by a thought she could have well done without: an image, clearer than any of the film she'd sat through tonight, of Johnny Cross stooping low over Isabelle Brooks, reaching for her hand, closing his fingers around hers.

"No, that won't be necessary," the detective said. "We already have a positive identification. Your landlord, Mr. O'Reilly, was good enough to—"

She heard very little of what followed. The noise in her head, harsh as a factory, drove everything else out. So it *had* been Joan: what else could a positive identification mean?

Therefore the hand she'd glimpsed, mottled and leathery as a pensioner's, had been Joan's. The realization was all too much.

The light bulb directly above Leigh's head swung suddenly down in front of her face, the walls spun about her. The uniformed officer caught her before she hit the floor. She hadn't blacked out, not quite, but for a while the landing and everything on it turned soft and hazy.

"Better get her to her room," someone said. "We'll talk to her later. See if there's someone to look after her if she needs it." The voice sounded distant as a dentist's. It bounced off the wall, bringing back memories. She was recovering from surgery, her mouth so numb and swollen, she didn't dare speak.

She was vaguely aware of the officer asking her room number, and the next thing she knew she was sitting on her bed staring down at her feet, a whistling noise between her ears gradually fading. The light was on, and about half an hour had passed, and at the doorway was the plainclothes detective, who must have let himself in.

"We're all about done here," he said. "Thought I'd check and see how you were coping."

"Thank you," Leigh said, and knew from the rush of feeling to her throat, her nose, her eyes that she'd been weeping. "I'm fine. I'll be fine in a minute."

"Wondered whether you'd mind answering a couple of questions, now rather than later. Save you having to visit the station." Before she could decide for herself, he began. "You've known Joan Bradley how long?"

"A couple of terms. Since last September."

"You met for the first time here in Bournemouth."

"That's right."

Dragging a chair from the table to the center of the room, he lowered himself onto it, facing her. "Were you about the same age, more or less?"

"Seventeen, yes. Joan I think was a few months in front of me."

"But you knew her quite well. How well?"

"As well as friends do. Better than some friends do, I'd say." Leigh shrugged tiredly. She felt light enough to float; she hadn't even the strength to wonder where any of this was leading. "We talked about all things; nothing especially deep. We didn't stay up nights philosophizing or anything."

"No, of course not. But you would have known if she'd been . . . involved in anything?"

"In what, for instance?"

"Anything out of the ordinary. Drugs, perhaps. Anything unusual. I'm wondering about the circles she moved in; the people she mixed with."

"*We* were her circle as far as I know. She had her moments, but don't we all? We all have late nights."

The detective considered this, his gaze narrowing and darkening until she felt the urge to look away. "You weren't especially aware of any change in her lately? Whether she'd been particularly ill? Not quite herself?"

"I guess so. Although . . ." Leigh shook her head, though briefly she had an image of Joan's haggard face, the blood-shot eyes, the almost too-white skin. "I suppose she seemed tired and overdrawn lately, but it isn't the kind of thing you dwell on. You put it down to no sleep or too much drink."

"Some of the residents have complained about noise. Can you comment on that?"

"Noise?"

"Disturbances. Loud music, loud voices, that kind of noise?"

What was he getting at? She felt a surge of anger, a sudden need to rush to Joan's defense. "Really, I don't see what she's supposed to have done. In any case, aren't you asking the wrong questions? As far as I know, she was like anyone else: sometimes she played music late at night, sometimes she went over the top. That's how she was. But she worked hard, she was bloody good at what she did, she deserved to relax, and what's wrong with that? It's as if you're accusing her of something. Shouldn't you be trying to find out what happened to her and why, instead of—"

"That's what we are trying to find out," he said. "You must understand, miss, that we have to examine every possibility. The *way* your friend died presents us with certain problems."

She couldn't bring herself to mention what she'd seen beneath the sheet on the stretcher. But she didn't need to. He'd already answered the question she'd dreaded having to ask. Whatever had killed Joan had done the same to Isabelle Brooks, and now she needed no convincing that what Johnny Cross had claimed was true. She'd seen for herself.

Unable to meet the detective's eyes, she stared at the carpet, momentarily losing herself in the tacky design. A numbness crept into her limbs, and she imagined herself sitting here and not moving for a week, doing nothing except stare at the floor. Her head crowded with terrors, with the awful thought of what might have happened if she'd reached for Joan's hand.

The scrape of the chair as the detective stood up brought

her back. Returning it to its place at the table, he reached the door before speaking again.

"Sorry to have to put you through this. I hope you'll understand why now, rather than later. And please believe me when I say your friend isn't under suspicion: we're genuinely concerned with what happened to her." When she didn't reply, he turned away, closing the door silently after him.

From her place on the bed she could still hear the crackle of police radios. The voices were no clearer than before. She heard one vehicle maneuvering and driving away into the night—the ambulance perhaps, carrying Joan. Seconds later she picked out the detective's solemn, emotionless voice again. This time he was outdoors in the forecourt, preparing to leave.

She wondered whether she ought to force herself up from the bed and chase after him before he could go, tell him what she'd forgotten to mention. In the end she hadn't the strength, and she stayed where she was. After all, would it really matter so much that she hadn't said a word about Graham?

· 7 ·

The killer arose before dawn.

Putting on jeans, boots and a faded denim shirt, he went down to the sea, to watch the waves advance up the shore as first light took hold. The front was deserted this morning, the way he preferred it, before the tourists came flocking. The breeze cut into his face and flapped at his shirt sleeves as he seated himself on the low stone wall above the sands.

Strangely, whenever he did this, he experienced a peace that escaped him at all other times. In some way the tide soothed him, helped him feel less responsible for his actions. After all, he couldn't be blamed for everything; that would be like—like judging the rain for falling, the tide for sweeping inland. It would be like judging lovers for falling in love.

He only did what he did because it was part of him, because he had no control of it.

Sooner or later the killings would end. They would have to. Someone would find him out, or he'd lose the touch or even the need. And it *was* a need, as if they would ever understand, and that was what made him a victim too. As much a victim as the others, as much a victim as the rock star Joan, or Isabelle before her.

Some distance away, perhaps a hundred yards out to sea, a pale shape turned slowly over in a wave and was gone. The killer froze, training his vision on the spot where he thought he'd seen it. Most likely it had only been foam. In this half-light it was almost impossible to tell. He relaxed again and looked east. From his vantage point, the gentle curvature of the coastline was such that he'd soon see Bournemouth highlighted in the sun, possibly even Boscombe beyond.

Where had he first met Joan? The rock star, he'd nicknamed her, and when she'd dressed in black, her favorite color, she had *been* a star, never mind looked like one. If she hadn't been a born photographer, she could have carved a career for herself on the other side of the lens. They were wild days with Joan, he remembered fondly. Late nights, early mornings, fast times, but that's what she'd wanted, everything louder and larger than life. He'd always tried to give her what she wanted.

But he still couldn't face the thought of their last night together. Joan's last on earth, the look in her eyes when she'd realized what he'd done to her. Had she believed him when he'd said it was only because he loved her? He sincerely hoped so, since that was the truth.

He stopped once more. Something—the pale shape at sea —had just flashed at the edge of his vision again. Straining to see, hardly daring to blink, the killer eased himself down from the wall until both his feet were firmly on the sand.

Whatever was out there was still trapped in the wave, the same wave that any moment now would break on to the beach.

He began striding toward it, wondering why he'd initially assumed it was foam. He'd been trying to blot it out of his thoughts, refusing to accept what it might be. Then why run down to the water to meet it? Shouldn't he be tearing in the opposite direction?

For a long, unreal moment there was silence on the beach. The waves breaking across the shoreline seemed to transmit no sound. He slowed as he reached the water's edge, fascinated and terrified. Miles distant, the horizon was turning a pale salmon pink. Nearer, perhaps ten or fifteen yards out, the thing he'd glimpsed bobbed weightlessly in the water. When the wave broke, the shape rushed wetly toward him, entangled in weeds.

It was nothing: an air mattress that had been lost to the sea and now found again. Most of the air had left it. In fact, it looked as if the weeds had choked it empty. He pushed it aside with his boot and turned away up the beach.

Until it had reached his feet, he'd been afraid to see what it was. What had he expected to find, though? That one of his victims had come back to claim him? Perhaps the first of many? A ludicrous idea, though it had crossed his mind daily and nightly for as long as he knew. On those nights when he did dream, this was his nightmare.

He strode back up the sands toward Poole, the breeze at his back. Suddenly he felt a deep-seated cold. Putting his hands together for warmth, he realized he was trembling.

· 8 ·

It had always been a habit of Joan's to pace restlessly back
and forth when the going got rough. This morning it was Sophie who couldn't settle. At least the apartment in Winton
she shared with Darren—the upstairs floor of a red-brick
semidetached house—was spacious, with plenty of room in
which to pace. Apart from the armchair and the brown cor-
duroy sofa on which Leigh sat, the only large objects in the
bright front room were the canvases Sophie had painted.
Two—a not very flattering self-portrait; a bowl of glossy
fruit—hung on the walls. Others were piled in a corner.

Sophie sat in the window seat, legs tucked under her. She
was still white with shock, her movements slow and dreamy.
As she took to her feet, a look of astonishment came over
her and she halted, motionless.

"What am I getting up for?"

"To make tea?" Leigh suggested. "To make water?"

"Neither, I'm sure. I've managed to do both about thirty
times already. I'll be damned if I know what I'm doing."

She flopped down again, encircling herself with her arms, dragging her knees to her chin.

Leigh, having slept hardly at all, had phoned just before eight with the news about Joan. Ten minutes later Sophie's Citroën had arrived in the forecourt, sweeping Leigh away to Winton.

"You know what this means, though," she said, as if what she'd been thinking was common knowledge.

"No. What?"

"Everything Johnny Cross told us was true after all. I misjudged him."

"Yes, but his story was so incredible. At least it seemed so at the time. Not anymore."

"No, not anymore. I assumed he'd imagined those things because he was such an emotional mess; I wasn't able to accept what Darren could, that Johnny was genuinely screwed up by what happened at the hospital."

"It isn't important what you *thought*," Leigh tried to assure her. "What matters is that someone or something did the same to Joan."

"Yes, but what? Joan asked the question herself that night at your place. What on earth could bring about such a change overnight?"

"Well, something did," Darren's voice boomed from the kitchen, which adjoined the front room. There was a clatter of pots, and a few seconds later he came through, balancing three plates loaded with steaming tagliatelle, his face almost blue with concentration. Having handed around the plates, he sat cross-legged on the floor in front of Leigh. "Not that we can outguess the experts, but we do know that something did happen to Joan, and the chances are it wasn't an accident or suicide."

"You left out murder," Leigh said.

"I'm not even convinced it was that. For one thing, both Isabelle and Joan were altered *physically,* as if the life had been drawn out of them. Forgive me if I'm wrong, but I don't know of anyone who goes around doing that premeditatedly. Something else touched them, for sure."

"*Touched* them?" Sophie was dumbfounded. "You're making it sound like some spiritual experience."

"Well, I don't mean to. It's just that . . . " Darren appeared lost in thought as he played his fork through his food. "There were reports in the national press a few weeks ago about something called spontaneous combustion. What happened was there was a series of farm fires in the north of England, all within a radius of about thirty miles, and within a few days of each other, and they were trying to establish the causes, or whether the fires were linked in any way.

"The first thing they were able to rule out was the climate. For one thing, two of the three fires were inside farmyard outbuildings; and this was toward the end of a long, cold, damp spell. There was no tinderbox effect.

"So the next assumption they made was that someone had started the fires, even though nothing of value was destroyed. Anyone meaning to cause serious damage could have done far worse without trying, and in any case the forensic tests proved nothing. So they ruled out arson. At which point the farmers more or less shrugged their shoulders, stopped asking questions, and filed their insurance claims."

"I really don't see—" Sophie began, but he silenced her with a hand.

"I'm coming to the point. Chances are this would never have made a story at all except for one thing. There was another fire a couple of weeks later. And this time an eyewitness, some old townie who was out in the country somewhere near Ingleton, birdwatching. He had his field glasses and his camera, and at some point he came within range of a farmyard.

"Well, what he told the reporter was that he'd started watching the yard because something there caught his eye. It turned out to be smoke. It was rising from a great mound of straw they'd brought out to the yard from the barn where they'd been storing it. Some of it would go into animal feed, some into manure for the fields. There was no one in the yard, and he was wondering whether he should report the smoke when the whole pile set itself alight. The way he described this was as though he'd seen a bomb going off—no warning, only a wisp of smoke and then *wham*!

"They can never know for sure, of course, but the newspaper reports concluded that all the fires—four in all—had been caused by stored energy. They'd combusted . . . spontaneously.

"Not that that's unheard of. Just that the investigators never put two and two together. After all, who'd expect it to happen so many times in such similar circumstances? It just doesn't work like that! It's easier to believe that some lazy slob dropped a match."

"I still don't see what you're getting at," Sophie said through her pasta. "How can stored energy blow anything up?"

Darren smiled wanly and put down his fork. "I'm a photographer, not a scientist. What I do understand is that heat sometimes collects and builds up inside a stored mass. It might be a living mass or an inanimate one. And sometimes it reaches a point where it can't check itself; there's no thermostat system to counter the rising heat."

Leigh picked at her food without appetite. Suddenly she thought she saw where Darren was leading. "You're going to tell us that this also happens to people, right? People like Joan and Isabelle?"

"Well, it has been known. People have been known to combust, to burn out without warning. After all, the human body has its own way of storing and generating heat. And sometimes the thermostat fails."

In the window seat, Sophie let out a gasp and put down her plate.

Darren went on, "I'm not suggesting that's what killed Joan, only that something triggered a reaction in her. It was either a process she caused herself, that built up inside her . . . or something caused it."

"She didn't burn up, though," Sophie said with a glance toward Leigh. "She—well, if she became like Isabelle, she got *older,* she shriveled."

"Which is also a way of burning up energy," Darren said. "Look, this is only throwing mud at the wall. All I'm saying is that something of this kind *might* have happened. If the body's temperature gauge can break down, maybe whatever keeps us young or allows us to age gracefully can break down as well."

"It's the suddenness that gets me," Leigh said. "The last time we saw Joan was—when?—I think the night you all came up to the Coffin after the hospital, and she was more or less her old self then. More or less. Yes, I know she looked like hell, but that was nothing new with Joan. You can't relate her appearance then—her heavy eyes and bad skin—to what happened two days later."

"Can't you though?" Darren was less than certain. "Suppose for a minute that what we saw in Joan those last few days were warning signs of a kind . . . the smoke before the bomb goes off. I hate to keep harping on spontaneous combustion"—across the room, Sophie winced visibly—"but in rare instances, people *have* been known to ignite, literally to explode, without notice. Things might have been building to that point for ages, even if it's seemed instantaneous at the time, and if . . ." He tailed off.

Sophie was off the window seat again, this time moving smartly about the room, collecting her bag from the empty armchair, searching out her sneakers behind it. "Darren, shut up for a while. Enough is enough. Does anyone else need some air?"

• • •

On the main street in Winton was a cafeteria named Giorgio's with tables outdoors on the sidewalk. On warmer spring and summer days it was possible to sit out and sip espresso and watch the traffic, while the smells from the fish shop next door merged with gasoline fumes.

"This is the life," Darren announced as a convoy of trucks thundered past, turning the air thick with dust.

"Fill your lungs, health freaks," Sophie cheered.

Leigh was suddenly laughing freely, enjoying the fact she

was able to. Thank goodness for friends like these. It was the lightest she'd felt since the night she'd met Stephen, though the moment didn't last, and how could it? Joan was still here, in spirit if not in the flesh. It was as if the cloud the trucks had sent up was the vapor, numbing everyone it touched. Sitting here, in the silence that spun out after the trucks had passed, Leigh began to understand what the vapor signified: it was the shadow that fell over every moment of pleasure, upsetting the best-laid plans, turning lives upside down, sometimes ending them.

Her own life was changing because of it—she was sure of that now. Why though, when for so many years it had been so emptily predictable, each day unbearably like the one before? Suddenly there was Stephen, the best thing to have happened to her, so right for her she might have invented him; and at the same time the terror, the memory of last night, two deaths sent to overwhelm everything else. It was as if one thing existed only to destroy the other. For every positive a negative. That was how the shadow worked.

Sophie was staring toward the movie theater across the road. A handful of customers was filtering in for the afternoon show, *Naughty Nina Does Bangkok*. She said with a shake of the head, "Why do they need that stuff? God help us." She turned back to Leigh. "Forgetting Darren's theories for the time being, what else do we know about Joan? Was she *into* anything that you knew of?"

"Strange you should ask," Leigh said.

"Why's that?"

"The police asked the same question last night. I've tried to think, but I can't honestly say she was into drugs, even if she sometimes tried to make us think that she was. That was just Joan trying to be hip. And certainly there was nothing I'd call weird, Ouija boards and black magic or whatever. We would've known if she'd been flirting with anything out of the ordinary. She didn't exactly keep herself to herself."

"Except for one thing," Darren said, "she was secretive enough about Graham, wasn't she?"

There were nods of agreement, but no words.

"I thought Joan was just being protective," Sophie suggested. "She hadn't been with Graham very long. And you know how things are at first: You want to exclude everyone else until you're, well, more familiar."

"I'll vouch for that," Darren said to Leigh. "Now that Sophie and me are used to each other, we're so boring we need other people around." He dodged aside as Sophie flashed an elbow toward him. "Maybe Joan *was* keeping him to herself, but how come we never heard a thing about him? Who was he? Leigh, didn't you ever meet him coming or going on the stairs? He spent enough time in her room, didn't he?"

Leigh could only shake her head. "They made enough noise down there, but we were never introduced, and I would've been intruding if I'd tried to say hello."

"Besides," Sophie said stiffly, "she more or less made it clear that she loved him, so who are we to sling mud? I mean, that's what we're doing, right? Sitting here looking for someone or something we can blame for Joan's death. Just because we don't know Graham doesn't automatically make him guilty, does it?"

Darren said, "Certainly not guilty; but he has to account for himself. Seems to me he must have been the last person to see Joan alive. So where is he now? Did you mention him to the police, Leigh?"

"Well, no, not really."

"Why not?"

"I . . . I don't know." Even in the clear light of day, she couldn't be sure why she'd withheld that. But she said, "Maybe I wanted to keep him to *my*self."

The others looked at her, at first without comprehension. Then the light dawned behind Sophie's eyes. "You're *involved,* that's why, as we're all involved. Because Joan was part of us and something stole her away before her time. And you want to do what you can; you don't want the police muscling in and pushing us out."

Leigh swallowed, tried to smile. She felt no relief, though Sophie had just put her thoughts into words. "The only thing is, there's very little I *can* do except watch and wait."

"You could take a look at her room," Darren said.

That stopped the conversation dead for a minute. Traffic rolled by, raising more dust.

At last Leigh said, "Why would I want to search her room?"

"Because you never know what you might find," Darren said, and Sophie said, "Even if you came up with something that led us to Graham, it'd be worth the trouble. If we could talk to him, we might begin to understand."

Darren went on, "Truth is, no one can say what you'd be looking for. First you'd have to find it, then we'd know. But sooner or later they're going to empty that room—her parents are going to claim her things and your landlord's going to rent it again—and that'll be that."

"Why me, though?" Leigh said, but she answered the

question herself. "Because I'm on the spot, right? I can come and go without being noticed. I was always in and out of Joan's place."

"All you'll have to do is figure a way in," Sophie said. "Do you think you can? I'll muck in with you, or Darren will, if it helps."

"No, I'll take care of it," Leigh said. "I might have to wait it out."

"But remember, the sooner the better," Darren urged.

"Today, then. I have to be there anyway. I'm expecting a call." It seemed the wrong moment to mention Stephen—the vapor would ruin the good news—and so she finished her coffee quietly before readying herself to leave. "I'll call you as soon as I know anything," she said.

· 9 ·

After Winton's traffic noise she was glad for the peace on Cavendish Road—glad until she came within sight of Silverwood Dene, and remembered what she had to do.

It was one of those memorable tranquil afternoons when time slows, peace descends, and summer makes its presence felt. The road was deserted, asleep. Only the leaves in the trees overhanging the road stirred as she rounded the cricket ground, where a preseason practice was going on. The gates were open and she could hear the occasional click of bat against ball. The peace was everywhere except in herself.

The nearer she came to the Dene—crossing the road, starting up the drive—the harder her heart seemed to work. She crossed the forecourt, hoping that no one noticed her coming. She wouldn't have been surprised to see the front door propped open and residents flitting in and out with garbage from the apartments they were spring cleaning. Even on bad-weather days the car freak who lived on her floor could be spotted on the forecourt, waxing or hosing down his MG Midget, practically whispering sweet nothings to it.

Fortunately it was all clear. The front door was locked, the MG nowhere in sight. Leigh still had to stop herself from digging into her bag for her keys as she reached the building. Instead, with a flourish, she clipped the bag shut, thrust it over her shoulder and studied the numbered buttons—seventeen in all—like a rash on the wall beside the door.

She hit the one marked "Proprietor," then waited. Her heart had jumped from her breast to her throat. It's only a small lie, she told herself; surely he won't see through you. But by the time there was movement behind the frosted glass and the door began swinging open, the lie seemed larger than before, impossibly large for anyone to swallow.

At first O'Reilly looked vaguely disoriented, as though she'd interrupted his sleep. The smell of beer and perspiration wafted off him. Seconds passed before he recognized her, and then his smile came automatically; it was almost a leer.

"Oh, it's you." His blue denim shirt was unbuttoned, his chest tanned and dusted darkly with hair. Leigh tried not to stare, but he was filling the doorway, pressing himself forward into the gap. "You're back early today," he said.

"Lost my keys," she said, so quickly the lie was out before she knew it. She rushed ahead before she could falter. "I wondered if I'd locked them in my room by mistake. There was a whole bunch. The key for this door, the one for my locker at college. I can't think where else they might be— God knows what I'll do if I really *have* lost them. So I thought, if I could borrow your master, I'd get into my room and look around."

She needn't have explained, since O'Reilly wasn't even

vaguely concerned. Turning, he led the way toward his rooms, down a narrow passage past the downstairs apartments at the end of the hall.

"Come in for a minute," he said.

She hesitated, but would only appear foolish by refusing. He was just bringing the master key, after all. His outer door opened into the kitchen, which was clean but thick with the smell of cooking oil. There were muffled TV sounds from the next room, sounds that became clearer as O'Reilly vanished into his living room, leaving her by the sink.

"Won't be a sec," his voice came back.

He'd left the adjoining door open, though from where she was, she couldn't see what he was doing in there. Instinctively she stepped forward for a view.

The living room was in darkness, the curtains drawn. The only thing she could make out was the TV screen, and what she saw there made her suddenly anxious to leave, with or without the master key. He was watching—or had been when she'd rung—a stag film, like the one that had been showing in Winton this afternoon. He hadn't even bothered to turn it off, not that he was in danger of losing touch with the plot.

She turned away, returning to her place by the sink. The smell of oil seemed thicker than before: much longer and she wouldn't be able to breathe because of it. No wonder O'Reilly gave her such bad feelings, if this was how he spent his private life, devouring porn. Presently he reappeared, master key in one hand, beer can in the other. When she reached for the key, he kept a firm grip of it.

"I'll come up and let you in," he offered.

"No thanks, I can manage."

"It really isn't done, you know, letting the residents loose with this. It's against regulations."

"Whose regulations?"

"Mine." He smiled broadly, letting go of the key.

"I'll bring it straight back," Leigh said.

It took her less than a minute to bolt upstairs, unlock Joan's door and head down again. At the foot of the stairs she rifled her bag for her own keys: evidence. Smiling with all the fake relief she could muster, she jangled them in one hand while returning the master to O'Reilly at his door.

"That was quick," he observed.

"They were right there in front of me when I opened up. On the table under the window. Don't know how I missed them."

"Let that be a lesson to you then."

"Hmmm." She started to turn away.

"Terrible thing about your friend," O'Reilly said then, and sipped his beer. "Terrible thing. You wouldn't wish anything like that on your worst enemy."

"Thank you," Leigh said, as if he'd given her something to be grateful for. "I still can't believe it. You looked badly shaken yourself last night."

"Who wouldn't have been, seeing her in that state?"

"The police said you'd identified her."

He nodded and opened and closed his fingers over the master key. "As a matter of fact, I found her."

"You found her? How did that come about?"

"Well, to be honest"— he leaned nearer, which made her instinctively back away—"there'd been complaints, sort of, about the noise. Some of the old folks, they've been missing their sleep for it these last few nights. So I had to go up there. When your friend didn't answer her door, I decided to look in to see everything was all right. And when I opened up, that was when I saw her."

He stopped and glanced at the beer in his hand as if it were tainted. From behind him came the sighs and the grunts of performers in the stag film.

"What did you see?" Leigh asked, not really wanting to hear the answer; not needing to. His expression was everything.

"I saw something I'd rather not think of," he said. "All I'll say is that you could just about recognize her as the girl who used to pay rent for that room. What did that to her, I wouldn't like to hazard a guess. Had to call the law myself. They said, when they'd seen her, there were similarities between this and another case they were working on. They told me not to repeat what I'd seen, but that's not so easy, not when—"

"When what?"

"When what you've seen is still there, when you try to set your mind on other things, even when you close your eyes." Suddenly O'Reilly was almost unrecognizable as his customary sleazy self. Briefly his eyes were glazed and far away. "But I shouldn't be bothering you with this. Only wanted to say how sorry I was, what a dreadful thing it is. You'd better go now," he finished. "It won't do any good to keep going over it. You'd better be getting up to your room."

It was the first time O'Reilly had behaved anything like normally toward her. She didn't know how to react. In some way it unnerved her more than his gloating, especially when she remembered, trooping upstairs, that after his show of emotion he'd returned to his stag film. How could you deal with a man with so many faces? How could you trust him?

The sooner she was out of this place, the better. The walls had been closing in for too long, but last night was the limit. She stood at Joan's unlocked door, fingering the handle. The only thing now was to get the chore over with. She wouldn't be able to rest until it was done, nor would Sophie or Darren. Hearing a door on the landing behind her, she stepped neatly inside Joan's room.

The place was a shambles, but no more than usual. Pop posters were aligned helter-skelter on the walls; piles of records lay clear of their covers on the floor. One of the discs, which sat amidst a flood of garbage on the dresser, had been melted and molded into an ashtray. At least Joan's bed was made, the sheets clean and neatly tucked. On the floor next to it was a cardboard box stuffed with stationery, old notebooks and sketchbooks and envelopes.

Leigh sat on the bed and drew the box to her along the floor. Then she wondered about fingerprints. Dared she touch anything? Surely she'd handled everything in Joan's room at one time or another; her prints would already be everywhere. She dragged out a handful of papers and cast them onto the bed beside her.

Sorting the stationery into piles, she had to remind herself why she was doing this. She mustn't forget it was for Joan, or she'd see herself as others would: as a snoop, poking about where she had no business. What was she looking for, anyway? When she found it she'd know, Darren had said. Could he have meant this letter, postmarked locally, or this one, an airmail envelope, mailed in France? There were scraps of paper no one in their right mind would have kept—memos about TV shows not to be missed; shopping lists, addresses that had been written down and crossed out.

One unaddressed brown envelope felt bulkier than the rest. She weighed it in her hand, wondering. It was only partially sealed, and as she tore it open, several color photographs tumbled into her palm.

She flipped through them casually. A blond-haired young man in sunglasses occupied center stage in every shot. Smiling in close-up, eating ice cream in a park, posing in front of a Check Your Strength machine at a fairground somewhere. With his square jaw and fit, broad-shouldered body he looked just like the type that might have appealed to Joan. Leigh couldn't place him, though, and didn't recognize the locations in which the snaps had been taken. They didn't look like anywhere in Bournemouth or Poole. It wasn't until she was returning them to the envelope that she noticed the message scrawled on the back of one.

> To Joan—
> *With all my love now and forever*
> *Graham xx*

She sat for a while, trying to keep the words in focus. As she did, she felt herself shudder uncontrollably. Something about the message itself, or the way it was written, jarred. Wasn't it just that she hadn't expected to find anything so soon and so easily?

So this was Graham—several pictures of him, at least— but was it enough? There was no address, no telephone number. Perhaps among Joan's other things, then. Leigh re-read the message before putting the photographs back into their envelope and the envelope into her bag. An address book she found in the box was unused, which was typical of Joan. Among several sheets of folded notepaper without envelopes were a grocery list, a selection of scribbled quotes that might have been part of an art history essay and—

Something was slowly dawning on her. She was almost afraid to let it. Returning to the first pile of letters she'd dragged from the box, she looked for the one with the local postmark. Its looping-lettered address clicked with her at once; why hadn't it before? It was Graham's writing, matching that on the back of the photograph. Identical, unless she was much mistaken, to the writing on the envelopes she'd received from Apollo Introductions.

Flutter-fingered, she tore out the sheet of onion-skin paper and scanned it. Again, no return address. Had he been keeping it from Joan, or had she known it well enough for him not to bother?

Joan, it read. *You'll say there's no need for these sentiments, but I wanted you to know that when I hurt you, it's because I love you. And sometimes because I love you I make greater demands than you can meet. That's because the more time we spend together, the more I need, and in the end I know that's asking you to sacrifice so much. If it ever becomes too much, you have only to say the word. But please don't expect me to say it. . . .*

There was more, but Leigh was loath to read on. The letter made her uneasy. No wonder Joan had been so haggard lately, if their relationship had been as emotionally fraught as this letter. Still, emotional highs and lows were one thing; they still didn't explain the burnout.

But perhaps nothing in Joan's room would. Besides, she'd pried long enough. Leigh returned the letter to the box, threw in the rest of the papers, and was getting up to leave when another thought struck her.

It was the handwriting again. Surely the Apollo connection was more than a coincidence. Coincidence happened only in stories. She stood at the foot of the bed, gazing about for inspiration, wondering what on earth she was looking for. Then she saw it amid the mass of bottles and overturned talc on the dresser.

It was Joan's jewelry box, a hand-made pine container that Joan had bought at a Lyme Regis gift shop last year. The carved lid was fringed with flora and fauna. Leigh shook it gently. Several small objects clattered inside. As soon as she flipped open the lid, she saw what she'd half expected to. Almost lost among Joan's collection of novelty earrings and finger rings, pins and beads, was a tiny ceramic bird in flight.

By the time she'd checked that the coast was clear and dropped the latch on Joan's door, her mind was racing. In her right hand she clutched the tie tack so firmly, she could feel it cutting her palm. That didn't matter though: the pain would keep her alert.

She crossed the landing quickly and started upstairs to her floor. Halfway up she had the impression of someone—a figure she couldn't make out—rushing silently down to meet her. It was her own shadow rising ahead of her; her nerves and the poor light did the rest. She needed time to think through what she'd found; the sooner she spoke to Sophie, the better. If she could just pull herself together for a minute . . .

Easier said than done. This house, with all its dark corners, had made it impossible for her to settle. Every door she passed looked ready to spring open suddenly. Each muffled noise hinted danger. Turning right at the top of the stairs, she felt herself shaking. Everything in the dim corridor looked gray and half focused, smothered by vapor. One of the remaining light bulbs flickered as she passed underneath it. There was an inexplicable smell of ocean salt in the air as she flung herself forward to her room.

The door was open a fraction. She could tell before she reached it. She might have lied to O'Reilly about what she'd done with her keys this morning, but she did remember dropping the latch when she left. It was so much a part of her morning routine—checking for her keys, pulling the door shut, testing it once or twice—she couldn't have forgotten. Which could only mean someone had been in her room.

Or someone was in there now.

The thought was a shock of cold steel moving through her. It kept her from running. Either her legs wouldn't let her, or she was past the point of turning away. After Joan, what more could she fear? She knew the worst, the most dreadful thing that could happen. She'd seen what it could do. Perhaps it was time to confront it. For an instant she stood outside herself, watching herself seize the handle, push the door inward, step into the room.

As she did, the ocean smells faded. She thought she heard gulls, but the sounds could have been imagined, and passed as soon as they'd come. For a moment she was so preoccupied with the sounds and smells that she hardly noticed the figure spread-eagled on her bed. As she pushed the door shut, the figure lifted its arms toward her.

Leigh turned sharply, the breath drained from her body. Then she recognized the face peering out of the dark at her.

"You bastard," she said, and switched on the light. "You scared me half to death."

"A nice way of saying hello," Stephen Roth said, sitting upright, throwing his legs off the bed's edge. "Do you treat all your guests the same way?"

"Only the ones who break into my room and wait in the dark to pounce."

"Sorry, I expected you'd be in when I arrived. I wanted to surprise you."

"Well, you certainly did that." She couldn't help but return his smile, though. He was beaming at her with so much enthusiasm, she weakened at once. He was automatically forgiven, and by the time she'd thrown her bag on the table, her fears had evaporated. "I still wish you'd called first, the way we'd arranged. My nerves are all shot as it is. How did you get in?"

"Used my burglar's tool—bank card, that is—for your door. Downstairs, I managed to slip in when one of the residents came out. That was an hour or so ago."

"And you've been making yourself at home ever since, I see."

"Oh, sure, you know me." His shoes were off and there was a blue-and-white hooped mug she never used on the bedside table. Now he looked critically into it. "Must have been napping. My tea's gone cold. Shall I make us another?"

She gestured for him to stay where he was, began refilling the kettle. "I'll see to it. *You're* the guest, as you say."

"I've missed you, Leigh," he said suddenly but matter-of-factly. "I've been thinking about you all day."

"Wish I could say the same about you. What happened

last night made it difficult for me to think about anything clearly."

"You mean all this fuss with the police? Anything important?"

"There was a death in the house." She was leaning against the sink, watching a bead of water hanging suspended from a tap. "A friend of mine, Joan, was found dead. That's what I came home to. I'd planned to tell her about you and me, share the good news, but instead I . . . I . . ."

She shook her head, knowing that another word would send her tumbling like a house of cards. She closed her eyes, doing her best to ignore the confusion of noise behind them, biting back the pain that was straining her throat. The water droplet thudded in the stainless-steel basin as Stephen reached her, circling her with his arms.

"Leigh, I'm sorry, so sorry." His voice was something she felt more than heard, a faint tremor of air at her ear. "If I'd known, I would have stayed. You must have needed me last night."

"I always need you," she said, turning toward him.

In the small box-room, the kettle's rising, amplified noise was like waves, surging against a sea wall.

"Tell me about Joan," Stephen said. "Tell me about everything you've been going through."

"I'll try," she said, and began.

• • •

They sat side by side on the bed while she went over it again. At times she felt close to seizing up altogether. The tears would come, her body would become one concentrated ache. Then Stephen, without a word, would squeeze her hand, urging her on, sharing his strength with her. He listened in silence, his face taut and expressionless. She told him as much as she knew: Johnny Cross's account of that night at the hospital; the link between Isabelle Brooks's death and Joan's; Darren's talk of human combustion; everything up to the point where she'd left Joan's room after searching it, clasping the prize in her fist.

Now she opened her fingers, presenting the bird for Stephen to see.

"Well? What does this say to you?"

He took it between his fingers. "Well, it's exactly like the one I wore to the party the other night and threw away in the restaurant. And you say you found this in Joan's room?"

Leigh nodded.

"But you didn't know Joan was a member of Apollo."

"She mightn't have been a member. She might've attended just once, like we did. And once might well have been enough."

"For what?"

"For Joan to meet Graham." Leigh broke off just long enough to search out the photographs from her bag. Stephen skimmed through them thoughtfully, gnawing his lip. "There was a letter as well, but I only kept these. Honestly, this is like—like looking at Joan's ideal. Sometimes when we stayed up late, Joan and I, we'd try to imagine the kinds of boys we'd most like to meet. We'd try to describe the pictures we had in our heads, the way our ideals would look. Just a silly game, but *this* was Joan's dream. The athlete, the superstar."

"Oh." Stephen looked up from the photographs. "And what about your ideal?"

For the first time since meeting him, she felt herself flush. "The point is, if she met Graham through the agency, she must have felt she had something to celebrate. At least it gave her what she wanted! That's why she made such a fuss about me joining when the application form came. After I threw it away, she even kept it for me. I really thought she was ribbing me too. And all she was doing was trying to help."

"If Apollo did her so much good, though, why didn't she tell you?"

Leigh shrugged. "Pride. The same reason I didn't want people to know I'd replied. Using an agency seems like an admission of defeat, as if you can't make your own way without."

"Maybe we can't," Stephen said.

"But we are, aren't we? We both recognized we didn't belong with that crowd. We didn't need what Apollo had to offer."

"But we wouldn't have met without it." Putting aside the photos, he took both her hands in his. "And maybe that's all Joan was getting at: she hadn't needed it either, but it led to good things for her."

"No." She shook her head stiffly. "It led to her getting herself killed."

At first she couldn't believe what she'd said. Was that what she really believed? Then she was aware of Stephen's grip on her hands slackening; for a second or two he stared at her blankly, still as a photograph.

"Can you be so sure?" he asked.

"I don't know. Perhaps not. But it's what I feel."

"What? That someone she met through the agency killed her? Someone *caused* her to burn out?"

"I can't be sure what I think. But there *was* a cause. Maybe it *was* a person."

"Graham?"

She shook her head weakly. Stephen let his fingers travel to her face, brushing a fallen strand of hair back from her brow. Though his touch was warming, he seemed not to see her, as if his mind were elsewhere. Finally he wondered, "Do you think we should take what you've found to the police?"

"Later," she said. "Not yet."

"You're not planning to conduct your own investigation?"

"I might be. Why shouldn't I? Why shouldn't *we*? Joan was my friend."

"That's missing the point. You don't know what you're dealing with." He was trying to help, but his words were making her adamant. "Remember what happened to the others," he added.

"I wish I could forget, I really do."

"Then why put yourself though this? Why take the risk?"

"Because," she said, and had to think hard. The horror had sucked her in; she had no choice but to go forward now. "Because Joan was a friend, and I owe her this much, and because I don't really care about what happens to me."

"But I do," he said. "I care."

"I know. I know you do."

He was cupping her face in his hands, facing her to meet his gaze, and she could feel her strength leaving in fits and starts. For now she was surrendering the argument and the search for truth. There was only Stephen, the room, the cool silence outside. The world revolved around this. In an instant, he'd changed everything, her whole way of seeing. The rest could wait.

"I'll help you," he said. "I'll do what I can."

I love you, she thought, not sure if the words reached her lips before he kissed her. She wanted the truth and would search it out for the sake of those who'd died, but it was something she'd deal with later, in its own time. Right now, with an urgency that blotted out everything, it was Stephen she wanted.

Easing her back on the bed, he said quietly, "Are you sure?"

"Never surer," she said, and for a short time her troubles were over.

· 10 ·

Stephen must have left before daybreak. She woke alone, still trapped between dreams and the real world. For perhaps an hour she lay in a tangle of sheets, reminding herself it had actually happened. The room turned uncertainly whenever she shifted her position in bed. Her head throbbed dully, her abdomen felt swollen and burning. Thank God, at least, for the weekend. Time to recover her senses, to throw off the veil of confusion and fear she'd felt closing in until Stephen had touched her last night.

At ten, after breakfasting late, she trooped down to the pay phone in the hall. It was part of the Sunday morning routine to call home, although sometimes she wondered why she bothered. Ever since her father, a long-distance truck driver, had gone to the woman in Kilmarnock he'd been seeing for years, her mother had lost interest in everything outside her own small, bitter world. A succession of new men had trooped in and out of her life, each more beery and uncouth than the last. She couldn't have been looking for love with them, could she? It was as if she'd been trying to liberate herself after so many years of drab marriage. If so, she'd been going about it the wrong way. She still insisted on sending money and hearing Leigh's voice once a week, perhaps to ease her conscience. She hadn't been able to pack Leigh off to college quickly enough when the time came.

"It's me," Leigh said as soon as the phone was lifted and before her mother could answer.

"Fine. Hang up then. I'll phone you right back."

Leigh replaced the receiver and waited. These calls always went on her mother's bill. The delay before the phone rang was sufficient for her to decide not to mention anything about this week, the fact that so much was changing. What her mother wanted to hear was that nothing had changed.

"Is everything all right?" her mother asked. "You sound as though you've just gotten up."

"It's been a slow start. Sunday morning blues, you know. One more day of bliss."

"That's right, spoil yourself. Don't overdo it, though. You shouldn't neglect your work."

"Thanks for the advice. What will you be doing?"

"You won't believe this, but watching a soccer game. Sunderland versus—I forget who else."

"But you *hate* soccer," Leigh said, astonished.

"Not anymore. Ralph is teaching me all the finer points. It's intriguing, once you get to know a few things about it."

"Who's Ralph? I thought you were seeing what's-his-face, Gerald, the pool player and alcoholic."

"Oh, Gerald was ages ago. Before Colin."

Leigh had never before heard of Colin. Her mother was

light-years ahead of her. "*I'm* seeing someone now," she offered.

"Oh, that's nice. Anyone special?"

"Mmmm. Quite special, yes."

"But you're not going to let it affect your work?"

As if you care, she almost replied. Instead she said, "It's too early to say. But so far it's been wonderful."

"Oh?"

"We share the same interests, even like the same writers and artists. He's mad about Cézanne."

"Uh-oh."

"It might even be love."

"I was afraid you'd say something like that." There was no trace of humor in her mother's voice. "Just be sure you know what you're doing, Leigh. You're very young."

"I'm pushing eighteen, Mom."

"In my book that's still very young. Which also means vulnerable. I wasn't much older when I met your father, and you know about *that*."

Did she have to judge everything by her own bad experience? "Sorry," Leigh said, "but this line's so crackly. You're not coming over too well."

"Nonsense. You always pretend not to hear what doesn't suit. No one's trying to stop you enjoying yourself. Just don't pin all your hopes on this boy, whoever he is. More often than not, you'll be the one who gets hurt at the end."

"But if it's good—"

"If it's good, then great. If it stays that way, even better. Just remember that sometimes you can give so much to a man, you've nothing left; keep something in reserve is all I'm saying. Otherwise—" She paused there, meaningfully. "You mind what I say, that's all."

Once bitten, Leigh thought. But we've all been bitten, and we all came back for more. You couldn't afford to let one sour relationship ruin everything that followed. Stephen had taught her as much. He'd had traumas of his own, but he hadn't allowed that to come between them.

Brightening, her mother said, "So how are your friends?"

Which effectively ended the conversation. One of them *died,* Mom, flashed through Leigh's mind. One of them had the *life* drained out of her.

But she said without emphasis, "Fine. Just fine."

"That's good. Send them my regards. And I'll speak to you next week, shall I? Same time, as usual?"

"Yes. Same time."

Hanging up, she felt a surge of both relief and frustration. There were people she could confide in, but for longer than she cared to remember her mother hadn't been one of them. It wasn't necessarily her mother's fault. What was wrong was that her life lacked passion these days; the men she took up with were such shallow nothings. It was as though, since Leigh's father went AWOL, she'd been purposely avoiding anything better, afraid of being hurt again. She hadn't allowed anyone to get close to her for years, not even Leigh.

Leigh gave herself a minute before dialing Sophie. A twinge of pain threatened to grow in her stomach, and her head reeled unpleasantly. In the midst of her discomfort was the ache she felt for Stephen. She could see his face clearly without concentrating. His eyes glimmered brightly; dimples formed in his cheeks as he smiled; he could do with a shave. Why couldn't he have been here to wake up with this morning? With a determined flourish, she stabbed out Sophie's number and waited.

After a dozen rings, Sophie answered, sounding still half-asleep. "Went and nodded off again," she explained through a musical yawn. "Darren was up and about bright and early. I saw him off and then crashed out. It's always worse, isn't it, when you fall asleep for the second time." There was a weary pause before everything came back to her. "Leigh! You never called me last night!"

"I had my reasons."

"Did you manage to get into Joan's room?"

"Yes, I'll explain all about it when I see you. Are you doing anything today?"

"Guess not. Darren's away with that reporter from the *Echo* again. I'd thought of going into town for a bit. We could meet at that nice vegetarian place in, say, an hour."

"Fine. See you there then."

"Leigh?" Sophie said before Leigh could hang up. "Is everything all right?"

"Sure. How do you mean?"

"Well, you sound . . . Never mind. Forget I mentioned it."

"Think I'm getting my period," Leigh explained, as if that were the source of all her problems.

"Are you sure that's all you're getting?" Sophie asked later, at a corner table in the Picnic on the Grass restaurant near the square. "Your color's all gone. You look dreadful."

"Well, thank you." Leigh smiled. "That wouldn't be surprising, would it, lately?"

"The box you're living in isn't helping. You never see daylight in there; ideal for a vampire, I always thought, but hardly anyone else. You're welcome to stay with us, you know, if you need a change. The sofa in our front room opens into a bed. It must be horrible having to be in that building at all after Joan . . ."

"It is," Leigh confessed. "You're right. It *is* starting to get to me. I'm even imagining things. A door opens on my floor and I'll jump! The wind in the trees outside gives me jitters. Last night I could have sworn I heard the sea, for crying out loud."

"But this is Bournemouth. You're near the sea."

"Not *that* near. Besides which, I spent *hours* last week painting something I knew was an abstract. It wasn't supposed to be *anything,* just pure feeling. And when I looked at it later, I realized I'd been painting waves, patterns of light in the water. How could I have done that without knowing?"

Sophie reached for a paper napkin, wiped her fingers, seized another chili taco. "Don't read too much into that, Leigh. Sometimes we get hyped up, we get lost in whatever it is we're doing and for a while the work takes over, and you don't see anything clearly. Since when did understanding what happens when you paint have anything to do with it?"

Leigh managed a smile. "Since you put it like that . . ."

"So much of what we do comes from"—Sophie waved her taco like a wand—"somewhere else, some private place we don't understand. You could call it the subconscious. When you heard the sea, when you *painted* what you did, it was coming from there. You were thinking about Isabelle and how they fished her out of the harbor. What are you smirking at, Taylor?"

"You're starting to sound like Darren."

Sophie rolled her eyes toward heaven. "Then we're finished. If we're becoming alike, what hope is there?"

They ate quietly and hungrily for a while, Leigh's attention taken by a middle-aged woman sitting alone at the next table, turning pages of a pink-jacketed novel entitled *The Perfect Romance.*

Sophie said, "Well? How much longer will you keep me in suspense? Did you find anything yesterday?"

While she listened, Leigh detailed her trip to Joan's room, producing the photographs, the ceramic bird trapped in flight. This time it came more easily to her than when she'd told Stephen. The hurt was still there, but now she was more in control.

Sophie's eyes widened. "You mean that jokey little communiqué from the dating agency, Joan got one too? And replied to it?"

Leigh nodded. "That's how she met Graham."

"Well, the old sly boots! I wouldn't have thought Joan . . . She never struck me as the type. I just wouldn't have thought."

"She might have been flirting," Leigh suggested. "Trying it on for size. In her case, something came of it. To be honest," she stalled briefly before plunging in, "I tried it myself."

"You? You wrote back? But I thought—"

"Joan saved it for me. She was determined I give it a shot, and now I see why. It worked for me too."

The novelty was sufficient for Sophie to forget why they were discussing this in the first place. Her face lit up and she studied Leigh as if for the first time. "Why do I get the feeling all my friends have been deceiving me? That's great news, Leigh!" Then, as an afterthought, "*Is* it great news?"

"It is. *He* is." She glanced up as a shadow passed outside the window where they were sitting: an elderly couple strolling arm in arm. "It would've been even better if we'd met at some other time, without all of this—" She waved her hand to signify everything; but her mental image was of vapor, thick as storm clouds rolling in. "As it is, Stephen—his name is Stephen—has only really seen me at my worst. I'm amazed he's managed to put up with me."

"Then it must be love," Sophie said half-jokingly. Her elbows were on the table and she was steepling her fingers under her chin. "Did you tell him about any of this? How did he react?"

"He thought I shouldn't pry. That I didn't know what I was dealing with."

"Which is true enough. None of us do. But . . ."

"*But,*" Leigh said, which seemed enough. It was a very large but. "There'll come a time when we take what we know to the cops, but not yet. First I want to find Graham. There's too much here that doesn't make sense." She indicated the pile of snapshots, which were heaped at Sophie's elbow. "These, for instance."

"What's wrong with them?"

"Probably nothing. Maybe I've done too much thinking and I'm not seeing straight. Who took the photographs, would you say?"

"Joan?" Sophie suggested.

"I would've thought so too. They're the kind of shots a lover would take. You have only to look at his face; he's in his element. He isn't posing for just anyone. But if they were taken by Joan, why would he add this message to them?"

Sophie's vacant expression prompted Leigh to go on.

"All I'm wondering is this. If he signed them, they must have been meant as a gift. In which case, who took them? Surely he wouldn't make a present to Joan of shots *she'd* taken. If they came from Joan's camera, why did he bother to sign them? You see the problem?"

"I think so," Sophie said uncertainly.

"Then there's the question of the handwriting." From her bag Leigh unfurled the original introductory letter from Apollo. Though the body of the text was printed, her name and the address of the party in Boscombe were clearly in Graham's hand. "Why would he go to the trouble of sending me this?"

"Joan put him up to it?"

"But it would've been as easy for Joan to address it herself, assuming she had the notepaper to begin with. She could even have disguised her writing if she didn't want me to know it came from her."

"I still don't see what you're getting at," Sophie said, and Leigh said, "I'm not sure I do either. Something here *feels* wrong, that's all. The passionate letter Graham wrote to Joan, the loud nights in her room, the fact he hasn't shown up through all this. You can see why Stephen thinks we should go to the police, but—"

"Perhaps there's somewhere else we can go," Sophie said, running her fingernail to the head of the agency letter. "This address is local, isn't it? Do you think they'll be open today?"

Leigh relaxed back in her seat, folding the letter, replacing it in her bag. "Probably not, but it can't hurt to try, can it?"

At the next table, the woman turned another page of *The Perfect Romance* and read on.

Five minutes later they were counting down doors along a narrow brown sidestreet off Old Christchurch Road. The first few houses here were of a formal, austere appearance. Many were private medical offices: dentists, osteopaths, electrolysists, all with brass nameplates affixed to the walls outside. Farther along the buildings were less well tended, their paintwork cracked and peeling.

"This must be it," Sophie announced, slowing outside an open door, beyond which were stairs leading up into darkness. They looked at each other uncertainly. There were no nameplates, though the faded number above the door was still legible.

"After you?" Leigh said at last.

"No, after you."

They thumped up the wooden stairs, their steps hollow and heavy between the walls. Their air had a musty thickness about it, as if dampness were rising from the foundations and no one had accepted responsibility for maintaining the place.

"Could do with a woman's touch," Sophie whispered with a nervous tremor on the landing, where the walls were unpapered and cobwebs coated the single bare light bulb. There were four doors here, which on closer inspection were three offices and a communal toilet. An accounting firm and a law office flanked the door marked Apollo Introductions. Seeing it, Leigh thought, So it *does* exist; unlikely as it sounds, it's real.

She knocked at the door and then waited. Sophie gnawed

a knuckle and shifted her weight from foot to foot until a voice behind the door called, "Come in, it's open."

"Now that we've come this far, what are we going to ask?" Sophie said, but Leigh was already pushing inside.

An imposing, broad-shouldered woman sat behind a desk smothered with paper. She had a flustered, breathless look that was emphasized by her hair, tied back so tightly behind her ears, it must have been painful. Fidgeting, she picked up and put down a pencil. Leigh immediately filed her as: forty, unmarried, sad, overworked. On a separate table was a personal computer, screen filled with innumerable file names. Another desk was similarly laden with scraps of paper, printouts, envelopes; a gray filing cabinet and a calendar still showing last month were the only other props in the office.

"Come right in," the woman said, composing herself as best she could. "You must be here about the job." Then she took one look at Sophie's green mohair sweater and pink leggings and turned her attention wholly to Leigh. "Are *you* here about the job?"

"No, not really. We . . ."

"That's all right. It's just that we're short staffed at the moment; I was expecting someone for an interview." She gestured at the mound of correspondence on her desk. "Just trying to get this in order while I waited. You'd be surprised how easily it gets out of hand."

"Well, we have the right place then," Sophie said. "This is the dating agency?"

"You could call it that." She laid a flat palm down on the papers. "More lost and lonely souls out there than you'd ever imagine. But you didn't come here to hear me talk. Are you looking for love, if not work?"

"Sounds suspiciously like a proposal to me," Sophie said.

The woman laughed quickly and easily, her face turning a deeper shade of pink. "What I meant was, are you wanting a form to fill in? Normally our correspondence reaches us through the mail, not in person."

"No, this is nothing like that," Leigh said. "We're trying to trace someone, and we were hoping you'd be able to help. It's quite important."

"He's a friend of a friend," Sophie elaborated. "They—they fell out of touch, and now we're trying to reach him. We think they met through your agency."

The woman reacted so slowly that at first Leigh feared she was ill. Her eyes flicked between Sophie and Leigh and she drew a deep breath, bringing her thick hands together like a schoolmarm preparing to sound off.

"There's a problem with that," she said. "You're going to give me his name and ask for an address, and I really can't help you there. We're obliged to protect our clients, after all. This is a very discreet business. You *do* understand, I hope; but I can't give out that sort of information left, right and center."

"We're not asking for left, right and center, just"—Sophie threw up her hands—"an exception."

"Couldn't you this once?" Leigh pleaded.

"The best I can do is this," the woman said. "It ought to be perfectly legitimate. Leave me his name, and if—I say if— he's somewhere in our files, I'll drop him a line to say get in touch. Can't say fairer that that, can we?"

Leigh glanced toward Sophie, who hunched her shoulders and nodded. Time was at a premium, but short of mugging the woman for information, what more could they do?

"His name is Graham," Leigh said to the woman, and then to Sophie, "Graham what? Do you remember?"

"Faulkner, I think." Sophie's face was pinched to a frown, one hand puzzling her scalp. "Or Fawcett. Or Faulk."

"Foulkes perhaps?" the woman suggested. "Graham Foulkes?" This was clearly a name that meant something. "You wouldn't have any idea what he looked like?"

"Here," Leigh had the photograph out in a trice. After the woman had studied it briefly, she wrinkled her nose and handed it back.

"Could have dyed his hair, I suppose, and he *is* wearing those sunglasses. But no, I'm sure that's not him."

"Not who?" Sophie said, vacant eyed.

"Graham Foulkes, of course. The one who worked here until about a month ago and left without notice. That's why we've a vacancy." She stabbed a finger toward the other desk. "And why the work's piling up. I owe him no favors, that slouch. Tell you the truth, I would have been forced to fire him eventually."

A silence fell. One look at Sophie and Leigh knew she was equally flummoxed. They'd come here to clarify, not complicate matters! Still, there was more than one Graham in the world, more than one Graham Foulkes or Faulk or Faulkner. She let out a sigh that she couldn't control. Why couldn't this have been easy?

"There must be another in your file," Leigh decided at last. "If you won't let us have it here and now, you could ask him to get in touch at this address." The woman wrote it down while she dictated. "Please let him know it's urgent."

The woman nodded, summoning a smile as if to say: If I could do more, I would. Placing the sheet she'd scribbled the address on squarely in front of her, she watched the girls to the door.

At the threshold, Leigh turned. "Nice party this week in Boscombe, by the way. But not quite *me*. Can't honestly see me becoming a regular."

"That's perfectly fine. It takes all sorts—" The woman stopped, slack mouthed. "Nice party where?"

"In Boscombe. On Sea Road."

"You must be mistaken." Searching out her desktop diary, the woman turned a few pages and said, "We do arrange informal gatherings once a month—always the first Thursday of the month, as it happens. So there couldn't have been one this week. And I don't think we've *ever* arranged a party on Sea Road."

Leigh opened her mouth to speak, but couldn't imagine what she should ask. Instead she followed Sophie back across the landing and downstairs, to the street.

· 11 ·

The temperature outside seemed to have risen several degrees while they'd been at Apollo. Pedestrians on Old Christchurch Road were peeling off their jackets and pullovers while slow-moving traffic shimmered in the haze the heat was creating. In one parked car a forgotten pet spaniel searched glumly for shade behind the vacant front seats. Because the beach would be crowded, Leigh and Sophie walked up from the center toward Horseshoe Common, the lush green island between the shops and vacation apartments.

Sophie said dreamily, "All I want now is to lie back and turn off and drift until this thing sorts itself out in my head. The more we learn, the less I understand. Are we going through shock, or what?"

Leigh stared as a shirtless youth, beer can in hand, stepped from a doorway in front of her without looking, almost sending her reeling. "Could be we're too close to see clearly, the way it was with my painting when I missed the overall. She *must* have been mistaken, mustn't she? Why would all those people turn up for a party wearing their stupid Apollo bird badges if Apollo had nothing to do with it?"

"Beats me. And since we're asking questions we can't possibly answer, does she really expect us to believe there are *two* Graham Faulkners, or whatever the hell they call him, both connected to the same agency? Isn't that too much of a coincidence?"

By the time they reached the foot of the island, Leigh was flagging. Her body felt like a dead weight as she spread herself out on the grass beside Sophie and lay flat on her back, face upturned to the sky. Closing her eyes, she could feel the earth hugging her, could sense the world rapidly spinning. She was utterly out of sync with it; if it ever stopped dead, without warning, she'd be thrown clear. In the momentary calm, the day and its traffic noise fading, the idea seemed quite feasible. If gravity should forget her for one second, she'd be gone. In her mind's eye she saw herself tumble through space, her body rotating slowly while a mist, impenetrable and gray, enfolded her. Would she hit the bottom of whatever it was she was falling into, or would the mist break her fall? Perhaps not the mist then, but the pale hands she saw rising from it to seize her.

It was the vapor again, so real to her she could feel it cooling her face. It covered everything, darkening whatever it touched. Opening her eyes, she saw a single white cumulus obscuring the sun. She hadn't been asleep, only daydreaming about dreaming. She heard voices, slurry and distant and unreal: three tramps on a bench nearby, plastic bags of booze at their feet, calling to passersby for money.

"Sophie?" she said, propping herself up on an elbow.

"Nnnn?"

"Why don't we go away when this is over? You and Darren and Stephen and me? We could go for broke and get a place in the country for a weekend, even a week."

"Nnnn." Sophie sounded closer to sleep than waking. "Sounds marvelous. We could take the car to the Continent." There was a lull before she mooned, "You're head over heels about Stephen, aren't you? Will we meet him soon, or are you keeping him to yourself the way Joan did with Graham?"

Perhaps Sophie didn't mean to make such a blunt comparison, but Leigh's first instinct was defensive. Graham and Joan might have been unsociable at best, but Stephen was different, and she wouldn't have him cast in the same light as Graham. Besides, they'd met only days ago; how soon did Sophie expect him to enter society?

"As a matter of fact he works near here," she said righteously. "I'll introduce him now, if you like." Before Sophie could reply, she was on her feet, striding away. "Wait right here. Don't you dare move. Then at least you'll have the chance to see that *he's* real."

She'd reached and crossed the main road before it occurred to her that her outburst must have taken Sophie off guard. Perhaps recent events were making her paranoid—and given the way her head was splitting and her abdomen aching, the way the traffic veered at her, no wonder she'd overreacted. Sophie had been making light conversation. How could she have taken her words as a dig? She'd apologize as soon as she returned with Stephen.

At the junction of St. Peter's Road the driver of a battle-scarred white Sierra braked sharply, hand on the horn, lips forming curses. Lost in thought, she'd looked the wrong way as she'd stepped into the road. Raising her hands by way of apology, she hurried on.

Still, she'd reacted defensively because the comparison had been there for the making, whether Sophie intended it or not. After all, hadn't she spent the last week following in Joan's footsteps? Hadn't her first encounter with Stephen been so easy, so perfect it might have been preordained?

She moved along Old Christchurch Road, past the liquor store, past a newsstand with handwritten for-sale ads in its window, dodging young couples strolling arm in arm. Farther along was the familiar yellow-and-red Superprint display. Through the door she saw Stephen serving a customer across a counter that was papered with ads for Kodak video cassettes. When he finally noticed her, he immediately called an assistant to take over and came marching out the door, arms wide.

At first, much as she wanted to hold him, she backed off. If he touched her now, she'd collapse, unable to say what she had to.

"You took me unawares," he said. "Is everything all right, Leigh? You don't look so great."

"I don't feel so great, but don't worry, it'll pass."

"That's why I left while you were sleeping last night. Thought you could do with the rest; you could do with a little more by the looks of you." He took a step nearer. "Are you . . . You're not beginning to regret what happened, are you? You don't think that's all I was after, because if you do—"

"No, it isn't that." She was holding herself back from him with all the strength she could muster, but this was only a formality; she only had to ask once and be done with it.

"Stephen, when we met. At the party in Boscombe. The first time you'd been to one of those things, you said."

"That's right. It—"

"Was it though? Were you really there for the first time?"

At first he looked as if he'd been slapped without warning. He offered the palms of his hands in a plea of innocence. "What am I supposed to have done?"

"You tell me. As long as you're honest, I don't care. If you were trying to make the right impression that night, I won't mind as long as you tell me."

His laugh was one of astonishment, without a trace of humor. "You've left it a bit late in the day for this, haven't you? What do you want to know?"

"Whether you'd met Joan before, whether you *knew* her, or saw her with anyone else. I don't know who else to ask, you see, or where to turn. If you knew her, you needn't be afraid to admit it; I wouldn't hold it against you. . . ." She tailed off, aware that she was ranting, crushed by the way he was staring at her.

"Leigh, I thought you knew me better than that. Why would I say a thing was so if it wasn't? You're not making sense."

"I know that, I know. Nothing else does, though. Make sense. It doesn't make sense that Joannie got herself killed, and Isabelle days before her, and that I should meet you and feel like—like I do about you so soon after, when I should be in mourning." The ache was everywhere in her now; in her lungs and throat as fresh tears began. She was thrashing away without rhyme or reason, a bull in a china shop. "I mean, why were you there that night on Sea Road when I needed you to be, needed *someone* to be? And why should it be so easy for us when by rights it should be almost impossible?"

"But it isn't easy, is it?" This time she didn't retreat when he moved nearer, drawing her hands toward him. "Look at what you're going through and what you're putting us both through, and think how much it hurts and how much you doubt, and *then* tell me it's easy. Christ, Leigh, you're trying to make this the hardest damn thing in the world!"

For a time they stood facing each other, not speaking, with the traffic rushing by and approaching pedestrians stepping off into the gutter, giving them the widest berth possible.

Stephen said, "Didn't I say I was there for exactly the same reason as you? That even after enough bad experiences to last me a lifetime, I was ready for more? So I came along looking for something special. Yes, I admit, I wanted this to happen. But no one can make it; who could guarantee you'd feel for me what I felt for you? You don't plan for that. We met and something incredible happened and that's all there is to it." From a pocket he brought a clean cotton handkerchief, dabbing her eyes with it before tucking it into her hand. "Now, you can end this right here and we'll both have to live with it. Or you can let me come through the bad times with you, and when it's over—it'll seem like forever before it is—we'll both be better people and everything will be so much easier, I promise, and the only reason we'll have is the one you're feeling now. You've already lost one friend; don't throw another away."

She couldn't be certain she heard every word, for her head was so clogged with pressure and noise. But she understood perfectly, and was reaching for him before he'd quite finished.

"I don't deserve you," she told his chest through her tears. There was so little strength in her, he was the only thing holding her up. "Why should you take so much crap from me and not bat an eye?"

"Because I know why you're saying it. I know what's on your mind."

"I'm sorry," she began, but he silenced her, touching a finger to her lips. She remembered the book the woman had been reading at the restaurant earlier—*The Perfect Romance* —and thought, Such things are never meant to happen, except in stories, and that's why I had to doubt and suspect and try to end it before it could truly begin. Stephen Roth was too good to be true, and for that she'd been punishing him.

When she'd calmed, she blew her nose into his handkerchief, took a great chestful of air and said, "There's someone I'd like you to meet. Someone I want to show you off to. Can you spare a few minutes?"

"Just point the way."

From Sophie's first reaction, Leigh knew there was nothing to apologize for. She only hoped her appearance didn't betray the fact she'd been crying.

"He's *gorgeous!*" Sophie announced, not bothering to lower her tone to spare Stephen the embarrassment. "Isn't it a pity we can't have two! Otherwise I'd steal him away from you and take him right home!"

"She's been in the sun too long," Leigh explained drily to Stephen.

They lolled in a semicircle on the grass, squinting into

the golden light. Nearby, the tramps on their bench were slurring, "Summertime, and the living is easy."

"If only," Leigh murmured, plucking up fistfuls of grass from the turf.

"Leigh tells me you know about Joan," Sophie said. Breaking the ice with small talk had never been her style. "She seems to think you'd rather we went to the police."

"Yes, because I can't see what's to be achieved by poking around without license. Surely it makes more sense to let them get on with it, especially if there's danger, and it seems to me that there *is* danger as long as you don't know what caused those deaths." He paused to look meaningfully at Leigh. "We wouldn't want what happened to those two girls to repeat itself. Besides which, you're high and dry. All you have is a name and a face, and nothing else."

"We have our loyalties," Leigh said. "The way I feel is: We're doing this for Joannie. It's our cause, and—"

"And we've been through all that," he cut her short. "You can still have your cause and your feelings, but let the cops have the photos, because as long as you're pussyfooting, there could be more victims piling up. If nothing else, the authorities ought to be able to trace Graham more quickly than you ever could, give him the chance to explain himself. And if you're still determined to nose around, go ahead, but without my blessing."

"Plucky little thing, isn't he?" Sophie said lightly. Then, to Stephen, "Tell me, how do we know that nosing around turning up stones is going to be any more dangerous than doing nothing? How do we know for sure that something else—*someone* else—was responsible? That this kind of thing doesn't simply catch up with you when you're least expecting it and bingo, like a heart attack! We were talking the other day about stored energy, people spontaneously burning out. Isn't that a possibility?"

"Anything's possible," another voice said, and they turned to see Darren approaching, backpack in hand, Olympus dangling from his neck. "Anything at all." Behind him, his lift, a Ford sedan with the *Echo's* insignia decaled across its doors, was just pulling away. He fell to his knees, breathless, disoriented. He seemed to take minutes before his eyes focused.

"Darren?" Sophie leaned forward. "You're not going to tell us it's happened again. Please don't tell us that."

He shook his head, wiped the back of one hand across his brow. "No, I'm not going to tell you that, but you're not going to like this any better. We were down at police headquarters just now, and then at the mortuary, in case there were any new developments. Well, there are.

"The alarms were sounded at six this morning. Sometime during the night someone broke in there, or out. Isabelle Brooks and Joan Bradley have gone walkabout. Their bodies are missing."

· 12 ·

It was getting so that you couldn't walk the Bournemouth streets without crossing paths with one newshound or another. They were everywhere: local and national, representatives of both the *Echo* and the *Mail* as well as reporters from TV and radio. Earlier in the day the killer had seen a film crew unloading itself from a BBC van outside police headquarters in Poole. Another television unit had passed by soon afterward, presumably on its way to the mortuary.

It had been like this since the weekend, when the story had gone nationwide. Now you had only to glance at the nearest newsstand to see headlines such as : "Linked Deaths Mystery Deepens" (*Mail*) or "Missing!" (*Sun*) or "Space Vampires Stole Corpses!" (*Sport*).

This last overstatement might have amused some, but not the killer. News of Joan and Isabelle's vanishing trick had made it hard, if not impossible, for him to see the funny side of anything. In truth, he had been in a state of bewilderment ever since hearing it. Unless there were stranger, darker forces out there than his own, it could mean only one thing. The Time was approaching.

He'd always feared it would, one day. After all, everything had a beginning and end, a dying day. But until now he hadn't needed to confront that fear, or ask himself how he might deal with it if it ever came to him. He had never thought of himself as mortal, only as ageless, a piece of time immemorial. He'd made headlines before, but never ones like these.

Seizing a copy of the *Guardian* from a stand near the entrance to the Pleasure Gardens on Westover Road, he walked on, ignoring the shouts of the vendor behind him. Ordinarily he would have hurried back with change, taking care to blend in, not set himself apart from the crowd, but today that seemed less than important. Picking up his pace, he walked through the gardens toward the boardwalk, where the waves were louder than traffic noise.

He'd turned several pages of the paper before locating the story the other dailies were running so prominently. It was tucked away among the In Briefs, as if the *Guardian* were embarrassed by the item it was running. The whole truth could be too much for some.

Folding the newspaper twice, the killer popped it into the first garbage can he came to, then continued to the beach. Of course *he* knew the whole truth, but how could he ever explain the need that was in him? Who would believe it?

Now the sight of so many well-tanned young men and women without clothing and the waves sliding high up the sands and then out again filled him with sadness like a physical pain. There was no peace here today, not with so much life and activity staring him in the face. He needed sunrise and the deserted sands, not this, the taste of death drifting in on sea air. To think of the suffering in the world, the fact that he was answerable for so much of it, to think of the lives he'd claimed down the years, unable in the end to stop himself from doing so . . .

But the sadness was as much for himself as them. He didn't want it to be over. That was the thing he most resented; the foolish need to search and destroy, the fear it might end one day. He stared out to the horizon, but there was no sign of the Time yet; only a speedboat churning up foam like an airliner's trail, and, nearer, a girl in a white one-piece swimsuit afloat on her back.

As he turned along the boardwalk, his path was blocked by a family of vacationers lining up for a photograph. A potbellied, sunburned Yorkshireman clutching an Instamatic camera was arranging his wife and two children with their backs to the sea.

"Nearer your mother, Katy, just another step, that's it. And Jean, would you just wipe the ice cream off her chin? No, *her* chin, not yours; you have none on yours. Would you look this way, Tommy? And wipe that bloody smirk off your face and try looking like you're enjoying yourself? Quick now, before the sun goes in. . . ."

With fixed limbs and fixed smiles, the family froze. The father squinted one-eyed through the camera, holding his breath and one arm aloft. For a second even the high puffs of cloud overhead seemed to stop—and suddenly the killer realized what he'd overlooked.

"Jesus," he said, so loudly the children's faces were turning inquisitively toward him as the shutter went off.

• • •

He arrived at the college shortly before midnight, entering through a small high window above a toilet. It helped that the lid was down; with a little effort he was able to lower himself onto it, and from there to the floor, without a sound. Fortunately the cleaners hadn't locked the washroom from outside.

All through the building were small, faint nightlights, one to each stretch of corridor. This was all to his advantage. Though he'd packed a flashlight, he could see what he was doing without it, which would lessen the risk of being spotted. Not that he could afford to relax, since places like this invariably had security staff who were liable to appear when least wanted.

Even in the half-light, the art department proved easy enough to locate. All he had to do was follow the wall-mounted paintings and the turpentine smells until he found what he'd come for. As he moved, his boots squeaked annoyingly on the tiled floor, their echoes seeming to go on forever, filling the vast empty building.

In a recess between two locked studio doors—both numbered, neither named—were the student lockers. There were forty or fifty in all, at least half of them open and unused. The killer stopped and dipped into his bag for help, retrieving a broad-bladed chisel, composing himself briefly before setting to work.

The locks were cheap token jobs; wouldn't stop anyone truly determined, didn't even make much noise. It would have helped if he'd known which was Joan's to begin with, though. It would have saved him the hassle of opening them all. Still, the break-in must appear convincing, as if someone had done this at random. As he cracked open one unsafe door after another, he felt himself breaking into a sweat. Suppose what he wanted wasn't here? Where else could it be?

At last, a dozen busted lockers standing open, he came to Joan's. He knew it was hers the instant he saw the slogan stickers peeling inside the door. *A word to the efficient is sufficient,* one said. It was her favorite one-liner, he remembered fondly. He could still see the twinkle in her eye when she said it.

But apart from a beach towel tied up like a Swiss roll and several contact sheets and prints of her favorite landscapes, there was nothing. He reached into the dark at the very back of the locker, but his fingers found only air. He picked up the towel and threw it down in frustration. Nothing rolled out of it.

For a long time, before leaving the way he'd come, he stood helpless, chisel still balanced in his hand. Nothing was going as planned anymore. Everything was falling apart. Perhaps this was one more sign that the Time was at hand, his number was being called. If so, he only hoped he wouldn't be compelled to destroy Leigh Taylor as well before it caught up with him.

· 13 ·

The first rush of dizziness came so quickly and without warning, Leigh was forced to grasp the nearest thing to her for support. As it happened, it was the canvas she'd been working on. The easel it was clamped to wobbled precariously but stayed upright. When she looked again, a smeared skeletal hand had imprinted itself over the waves, or was rising from them.

She blinked and tried to focus on what she'd done. The painting studio spun almost imperceptibly about her; it was a wonder that Tim Wright, her tutor, kept his balance as he came wading toward her across the tilting floor.

"Leigh?" he said. "Are you all right? What's the problem?"

There were only three others in the class this morning. All stopped what they were doing to turn and stare.

"Waves," she said, and looked at the metallic blue palm of her hand, and then again at the canvas with Isabelle's corpse trying to rise from it.

"Waves?" he repeated, frowning.

But she was only describing what was rushing forward in her head again: a pressure full of blackness and adrenalin, the power of approaching unconsciousness.

"Waves," she told the blurred dim figure that she knew was Tim, and keeled forward.

This time she didn't think to grab hold of anything. She had the vaguest sense of the easel coming down with her, and firm hands picking her up from where she'd landed, though she couldn't be sure of anything in between. She didn't remember hitting the floor or causing the graze on her knee that she saw when she looked again. It might have been there for days, for all she knew, except that the red looked fresh.

She raised her head, which felt twice its usual weight, and stopped. For a moment she'd forgotten where she was.

Across the desk from her, Dr. Jameson closed his file and nodded in private agreement with himself. He was fiftyish and jowled, and his large, sympathetic brown eyes behind thick-lensed spectacles made her think of Owl in the Winnie-the-Pooh tales. She had registered with him soon after moving to Bournemouth, though this was the first time she'd needed to visit.

Jameson said, "You'll be pleased to hear that we're not dealing with anorexia—you can even treat this yourself if you promise to *eat*."

"But I have been eating."

"Not enough of the right things, I'd say. Away from home for the first time? Student? My guess is you're living on junk food." She was about to object, but he pressed on regardless. "You're certainly underweight for your size. Do you bother to check your weight frequently?" She shook her head slowly. "So you wouldn't know when this began." His fingers searched out a ballpoint pen, which he held poised above his prescription-slip pad. "You're also badly deficient in iron and vitamin B_{12}. In fact I want you to eat all the raw meat you can lay your hands on."

She laughed and sneaked a look at her fingers, with their too-visible knuckles and joints and cuticles like baying moons.

"I'm trying you on a high protein diet," he said, scribbling illegibly for a minute before tearing out two separate sheets. "I don't usually do this, but I'm suggesting a number of good, stodgy carbohydrates as well. Punish yourself if you have to, then come see me in, say, a month. And you'd better have fattened yourself up by then or I'll be forced to put you on a cholesterol drip."

"Thank you doctor. I'll do my best."

Handing her the slips, he laced his fingers together and relapsed in his chair. "The first is a course of iron tablets: I want you to keep to it or we'll be talking pernicious anemia before long. Is that understood? The second is for you; if you can read it, you'll know how to prioritize your shopping from now on."

She accepted with thanks and stood up. Even now she felt uncertain on her feet. The floor wavered impossibly far below her; her head still felt like the inside of a shell that held the sea's roar.

"And take a few days off," Dr. Jameson said, rising, seeing her to the door. "I'm sure your college won't deny you the rest."

"But there's work to do. I *like* what I do, doctor."

"Then take your work home with you for a while. Didn't

you say you were at Art and Design Foundation? What's wrong with taking your sketchbook to the beach, filling your lungs with sea air? You're privileged to be living where people come to recuperate; don't want you doing it all in reverse, do we?"

In the waiting room she saw Sophie—dependable old Sophie, who had driven her here straight from college—rising to meet her as she came out.

"What did he say?" she demanded before Leigh could draw breath.

"He thinks I should take time off, do my work at home. I don't think I want that."

"Never mind what you want. We'll get your things."

Later, as they drove back from the Tech, the Citroën's rear seat lumped up with canvases wrapped in tarpaulin, Sophie said, "If you like, we can take this stuff straight to my place. You can stay with us, work there during the day. Hell, you could even move in! There's no spare bedroom but more space than you have now. And I'm not just talking about until you're better. You could stay until you find a place with Stephen. Have you talked about moving in with him yet?"

"Not yet. The timing would be wrong just now."

Too much was changing too quickly, and not only the everyday things. Even her body seemed to be running out of control. She was losing touch with it, as if it belonged to someone else. Her blackout today must have been a warning to slow down, perhaps even to put distance between herself and her situation. Though she had no doubts about being with Stephen, too great a commitment too soon might ruin everything. Better to wait for the horror to resolve itself, if it ever did.

As Sophie reached the Wimborne Road traffic circle, Leigh remembered that Stephen was the reason she had to be back at her apartment.

"He's picking me up tonight around eight," she said. "Would you believe he wants a romantic barbecue supper on the beach tonight? Just the two of us? Food, wine and moonlight?"

"Good grief! Darren never suggests anything like that. He'd better get his act together or he's *out,* believe me."

"Could I have him drop me at your place later? Or I could come around in the morning instead."

"Sure." Sophie went into her second circuit of the circle, finally exiting without a signal. The car behind drew up sharply with a screech, and several horns blared. Oblivious, Sophie said, "Just be sure you're in bed early, though. By which I mean get your rest."

"I know damn well what you mean."

As they passed the graveyard on their left, seconds later, it occurred to Leigh that ever since the weekend they'd been whistling past it, avoiding all talk of the tragedy. Darren's news had sent everyone into shock, after which all speculation seemed useless. Who cared how and where and when Joan had met Graham when what really mattered was that some nut case was stealing corpses from police custody? Did it matter who did the nosing around as long as the bastard was apprehended, and quickly?

Suddenly, in the light of this new revelation, the idea of withholding evidence, if that was what the photographs were, seemed foolish. And so they had driven to the police station with the prints and a garbled explanation. Fortunately, the desk sergeant hadn't questioned why they'd been so late coming forward. In the end, it was more important to make sure the prints would be circulated. Graham's face had to be everywhere.

At the time, Leigh had been so relieved to be rid of them, it had felt like a burden lifted from her shoulders. She'd hoped she'd be able to pick herself up again, put everything behind her, move on. But the trauma had taken so much out of her.

And now, as Sophie brought the car around onto Cavendish, another doubt struck her, a thought that didn't make her feel better at all. It had first crossed her mind as she had stood before her painting today, seconds before blacking out. As the pale, ethereal hand rose from the waves—a handprint she'd put there herself—she'd realized that something more than stress was stealing her health. Could it be the same thing that had stolen Joan's life, draining her until there was nothing left? Whatever it was, it was still out there somewhere: silent, invisible, deadly. And, she thought with a shudder, still hungry. Tell *that* to the doctor and see what he prescribes.

O'Reilly was out front when Sophie drew in at the Dene. It was another warm midafternoon and he was naked to the waist, wringing a chamois cloth into a brimful bucket as he worked his way around the downstairs windows.

"You'd think he'd pay someone to do that," Leigh said, and Sophie said, "You know why he doesn't. Because he gets off by gawking at other people. He's having the time of his life."

"I doubt it; most of the downstairs residents are over sixty." Even so, Leigh remembered all too well what he'd been getting off on last week. "Did you know he spends his days watching porno movies?"

"Wouldn't put anything past him," Sophie murmured. "He's another good reason for clearing yourself out of here, if you ask me. Didn't I tell you about the time he tried his luck with me, when I was up in the Coffin?"

"No."

"It's something and nothing really." Sophie reversed the Citroën into her usual spot and stared toward O'Reilly, shaking her head. The sun was at the point where sycamore shadows were beginning to crawl across the forecourt from the west. "Look at him sucking his stomach in for us! Because he spends all *his* time gawking, he thinks everyone's returning the compliment." She turned to Leigh again. "Well, he burst into my room once while I was still half dressed from the shower; only had a thin damp towel around me, and suddenly he's unlocking the door and standing there. I couldn't believe it, but he didn't apologize and leave, he just stood there wide-eyed and said, Sorry, didn't realize you were in; just came in to check the something or other, I can't exactly remember what."

"God," Leigh said, "the nerve."

"You could still hear the water in the bathroom draining. He knew damn well I was there, him and his damn master key. For all I know, he could've been perched around the corner waiting for his chance. I could've *killed* him for that. But to be honest, right then, I didn't know what to expect. I was scared, Leigh, I could feel myself shaking. In the end he sort of grunted and backed out; not too bloody soon."

"That's just what I need to hear before I head inside," Leigh said.

"Whoops." Sophie put a hand to her mouth. "I didn't mean to time it like that. Shall I stay until Stephen arrives?"

"Of course not. I'll be fine—provided I don't take a shower." Leigh forced a laugh without really feeling it. "Don't worry: he may be an oddball, but you should have heard him talking about Joan. It was the first time I realized he had feelings. I'm sure he's all right at heart."

But she sounded more confident of that then she felt. She had never really believed it.

"Should I keep your paintings?" Sophie asked when Leigh was half out of the car. "You won't be working here, will you?"

"No, but I'd like to show them to Stephen—he hasn't seen anything I've done. I'll bring them over later."

Waving the Citroën farewell as Sophie swung it back onto the road, she turned toward the house, hitching her canvases more comfortably into her armpit. She knew without looking that O'Reilly had stopped what he was doing to watch. In the silence her steps across the asphalt seemed almost comically loud, the distance between herself and the house enormous. For a long moment everything, including her breath, was suspended. Even the birds had fallen silent.

Fortunately someone had propped the front door open. This time she didn't have to fumble for her key. She hastened along the hall, not bothering to check the mail. A door creaked open to her right as she passed. Turning, Leigh found herself staring at a gray-eyed old lady who must have been eighty, if a day. There was a look of total incomprehension about the woman, as if she couldn't fathom why she'd opened the door. Her mouth twitched; a thin line of saliva dribbled to her chin. Finally she gave up and backed into her room again.

Joan, Leigh thought before she could stop herself. But that was ridiculous. She'd seen this woman coming and going as long as she'd been at Silverwood Dene. Even so, Joan must have looked something like that at the end; one glimpse of her withered white hand had told Leigh as much. She might have passed for any one of the downstairs residents, her flesh as mottled and lined as old rags, the life drawn from her as if—

At the foot of the stairs Leigh hesitated. No, what she was thinking was too incredible. All the old-timers confined alone to their ground-floor rooms, and O'Reilly lording it over them, bleeding them dry for rent to the end of their days when by rights they should be in care. O'Reilly, whom she had never trusted without knowing quite why. O'Reilly, who had found Joan's body, the first to see her in death.

And perhaps the last to see her in life.

Suddenly her thoughts were racing ahead like a fresh wave of dizziness. She stumbled to the stairs, trying to adjust her canvases, which had doubled their weight and were now threatening to slide free of their tarpaulin wrap. No, she thought, O'Reilly had his quirks and he wasn't to be trusted, but he couldn't have reduced his residents to this.

She needed to lie down and clear her head of such wild ideas; otherwise she'd be the next one they carried away, in a straitjacket if not on a stretcher. Sophie was right about this place; it was driving her over the edge, making it impossible for her to pull herself together. Somewhere behind her she heard the metallic thump of O'Reilly's bucket, then the slop of water down the nearest convenient drain. Glancing over her shoulder, she saw his silhouette at the doorway, the afternoon sun directly behind him, his shadow extending indoors along the entrance hall.

Leigh felt herself go numb. God help her, Sophie would be miles away by now. Why on earth hadn't she called Stephen at work and arranged to meet him in Winton—anywhere but here? She couldn't go back now, not with O'Reilly blocking the way. Besides, she hadn't the strength. Even without the canvases, she wouldn't get far. As O'Reilly put the bucket down and took his first steps into the hall, she forced herself up the stairs.

She was amazed she could move at all. A terror she'd felt only once before—the instant she'd understood how Joan had died—washed over her again. Her nerves were knives, driving her upward, away from the solid progress of O'Reilly's footsteps. She hadn't time to catch her breath; didn't pause as she reached the first landing but hurled herself off to her left, up the second flight.

Not that she could stop herself, but wasn't this exactly what O'Reilly wanted? He was driving her up to the Coffin, where perhaps in a way she'd always belonged. Was life so cruel as to finish her there, alone and uncared for in a room without light, to live and die there, as the old folks downstairs were living and dying?

As she reached her landing, she thought she heard the sea once more, a slow and steady passage of sound that supposedly inspired poets, lulled convalescents back to full health. If only it could do something for her! It faded, though, as she reached her room, became just one of many sounds in her head. Unlocking the door, throwing herself in and dropping the latch, she tossed her paintings aside and staggered back on her heels.

His footsteps never came. The knock at the door never came. Leigh faltered, barely able to keep herself upright, as if there were space enough in this dump to fall. Outside, the birds were still silent, the trees breezeless. After she'd stood alone with her heartbeat, listening, for fully five minutes, she decided that O'Reilly hadn't followed. The house was so quiet, she would have heard him coming, and he wasn't the kind to tread lightly. Jackboots, maybe; soft-shoe shuffles, not likely.

So what was he doing? Biding his time, safe in the knowledge he had her trapped? The bastard was probably enjoying himself. Well, she could bide her time too. She'd wait until Stephen arrived and then walk from this place forever.

That was assuming that Stephen arrived *first,* though.

Jesus, she must stop thinking like this; she had to keep herself motivated. Switching on the wall-mounted TV for noise—King Kong had just toppled from the Empire State building; "It was beauty killed the beast," an onlooker said —she flipped channels for the news and began packing. Fumbling her suitcases from under the bed, she began throwing in jeans, blouses, underclothes, in no particular order. As she did do, she noticed how the tarpaulin sheet had fallen partly away from her paintings when she'd thrown them down. For a second it looked as though the imprint of her hand on the waves had peeled it back.

Next she searched out a handful of Safeway shopping bags and began stuffing into them all her possessions— the ash-tray she'd made, her books and files full of art history notes. I'm really leaving, she thought; and what's more, I'm not letting *him* stop me. Whatever he'd done to Joan and Isabelle and God knew how many others, he wouldn't repeat it with her.

Could she really be thinking this? Perhaps paranoia had finally won her over completely. She couldn't be sure what she thought anymore. She glanced at her watch—just after six—and wondered how long before Stephen would arrive.

For the next few minutes she was so lost in packing, she almost missed the report on the killings. At first she was vaguely aware of what the newscaster was saying: "The search still continues. . . . Police are still baffled," and so on and so on. Then, half turning to the TV, she saw the face and stopped dead.

It was Graham. The face in the snapshots she'd turned in to the police. Except what she saw on the screen wasn't a snapshot but live-action footage of Graham walking straight toward the camera. In the foreground were journalists clutching microphones and photographers jostling for position. Behind Graham were steps leading up to a police-station entrance. So they'd finally caught him, and now he was going to explain himself! Well, it had better be convincing. Leigh flopped on her bed to watch and realized she'd missed the point completely.

His name was not Graham at all but Jonathan Barnes. At least that was the name that appeared as a caption as soon as he started speaking. He was reading a prepared statement, the first lines of which were drowned by the reporter's voice-over.

At midday today, Barnes had been at home eating lunch in front of the TV news when his snapshot had flashed on the screen. The story the *Sport* had described as the Space Vampire Horror had been a national headline since Sunday, when the bodies of Joan Bradley and Isabelle Brooks had vanished, and yet this was the first he'd heard of it. Because he'd been out of the country until midevening yesterday, he'd been astonished to find himself the prime suspect in a case that couldn't even be described as murder. He'd put down his knife and fork and driven at speed to the police station in Barrow-in-Furness, where he lived and worked.

The rest had been a matter of course. Everything he'd told the police had been checked: his passport; airline tickets; receipts from hotels in Tuscany and Bologna, where he'd spent the last month. Now, having read his statement, he was telling the reporters:

"Of course I bear no grudges. It's enough for me to clear this thing up before it goes any further. And no, I haven't any idea how my face came to be linked with this Graham Foulkes, though I'd like to know where you came by that photo of me." While journalists fired several involved questions at once, he brought out the shades he'd worn in the snapshots and put them on. "Sorry, but there's really nothing to add. Never been to Dorset in my life. And I can't comment on something I know nothing about."

Thanking the mob, he headed away. No sooner had he exited screen right than the TV snapped itself off, and the room plunged into darkness. Leigh remained fixed to the fading blue dot in the screen, hardly aware that the electricity meter had run out and needed change.

But if *he* isn't Graham, she thought, and forced herself wearily up. If *he* isn't Graham . . .

She was either too numb or too tired to react quickly when she heard the commotion behind her, felt the cool through draft from the window that meant someone was entering her room. When she finally did turn, the door was still swinging inward. It seemed an age before it was open all the way. Long before that, she picked up the scent of freesias, her favorites. Stephen!

But it was O'Reilly's face she saw, leering around the huge spray of flowers he was holding.

"I brought you these," he said proudly.

· 14 ·

When he first checked the negatives he'd processed, Darren just stared at them, perplexed. Two of the five rolls of Kodak Tri-X Pan he'd put through his developing tank and hung up to dry were all barren coastlines, automobile grave-yards, condemned buildings, nothing to do with him. The rest were familiar enough, having been taken on Sunday when he'd been with Dave Hunt from the *Echo,* though none had been needed for publication. It was almost five thirty before he remembered whose films he'd been handling.

By then the Tech had practically emptied itself out. In the cafeteria a handful of lecturers argued about how best to run the college and who should be running it. In the corridor outside the head office, two drama students were testing each other on lines from *Waiting for Godot.* Almost everyone apart from the photography students had gone. Sophie had abandoned the ceramics workshop hours ago, and was prob-ably still nursing Leigh, or helping her move things to Win-ton.

Darren strode to the photography department. A girl stood in front of the new dry-print machine, watching her work emerge on the conveyor as if witnessing some miraculous birth. Darren went to the locker where his negs hung and, with scissors, began cutting them into shortened strips before fitting them into plastic sleeves. As he did, he had a sudden clear picture of Joan pressing two rolls of film into his open hand, saying, "Darren, be a love and put this through processing with yours. I won't have time—I'm supposed to be meeting Graham tonight."

But, of course, barren coastlines and houses fit for demolition had always been Joannie's style. They must have been taken not long before she died, most likely the last time they'd been out on location. Jesus God, to think when she'd taken them how near she had been—

He pushed the thought away. It still hurt to go over it. What everyone needed now was distance, a chance for wounds to heal and the pain to die down. But we'll never forget, he thought, we'll never stop crying for justice. Would it hurt if he kept the negatives for old times' sake? They wouldn't mean anything to anyone else. Seizing a strip of Joan's film, he made a cut.

The first half dozen frames on the roll were not coastlines but a man's face in medium close-up. In fact, these must have been the end of the roll, not the start of it. Holding them to the light, he noticed how unlike the photos they'd turned in to the police these were. For one thing there was none of the jokey posing or muscle flexing. These had been taken indoors, mostly without the man's knowledge; in one shot, aware of the camera, he was raising a dark hand to blot out the lens as if unhappy to be photographed. Oddly, he didn't look much like Graham. But of course Darren wouldn't recognize the face in negative, not with its shock of white hair and pale-gray highlights where the eyes and mouth should have been. Make a positive of it and it might make more sense.

The department's darkroom area was partitioned into six separate booths, each with a bench and a Durst enlarger. The dryprint system had banished the smell of chemicals forever, at the same time putting a stop to experimentation and risk taking. Everything was so mechanical now, but that was the way the industry had gone. Finding the first two booths occupied, Darren took the third, fumbling in the dark for the enlarger's plug and the wall socket. He was rolling the strip of negatives into place when he sensed movement behind him.

"Darren? That you?"

Through gritted teeth, he said, "Yes, got it in one guess."

The voice and the unmistakable smell of Aramis—who daubed themselves with aftershave for *college*, for crying out loud?—were Rob Young's. It was well known that Rob's role in life was to be beautiful. Always well groomed, well shaven, immaculately turned out. It was also his role to borrow: change for the coffee machine, film stock, camera lenses, anything that wasn't nailed down would do. Before he could say another word, Darren turned on him.

"What do you *want*, Rob?"

"Who, me?" There was a hollow thump as Rob slapped an innocent hand to his chest. "Did I say I wanted anything? Actually this was only a social call to see what you were up to. And to see if you had a couple of spare sheets of photographic paper while I was about it."

"There'll be some in my locker. You'll have to wait until I've done this." Darren returned to the enlarger and switched it on. A rectangle of light appeared on the bench beneath the lens. The image was a smear.

"It's out of focus," Rob explained helpfully.

"I can see that," Darren replied.

"It's all right, I can wait for that paper until you're done."

"I know you can wait, Rob. You have no choice."

Darren brought the image on the bench into focus and stared, perplexed, at the face staring back at him. For an instant the dark seemed to swarm, worsening his confusion, and he was tempted to check if he'd inserted the right strip of film. This wasn't Graham—at least not the Graham whose likeness they'd delivered to the police.

Then Rob was nudging shoulder to shoulder with him, the smell of his aftershave intensifying. "Hold on. Just hold on a bloody minute. I know this fella. I've seen this bastard before."

"What?" Darren said, distracted, at first hardly aware that Rob had spoken. "What did you say?"

"That I'd know this bastard anywhere. This is the one who took off with Isabelle that night in Branksome Park. Stole her right from under my nose. Didn't I tell you? The night before they plucked her out of the bay. Where'd you get his photograph?"

"Excuse me," Darren said, brushing Rob Young aside as he hurried from the booth, not even thinking to switch off the enlarger as he left. In the foyer near the main office was a pay phone. He closed his eyes briefly, summoning up Leigh's number at Dene, then dialed. After twelve or thirteen rings there was still no reply. Darren thumped down the receiver and fled.

At first, his head spinning, he couldn't be sure what he feared or why he needed to run. By the time he reached the bus stop on Wallisdown Road, however, he was beginning to understand—and to panic.

· 15 ·

God damn it, Leigh thought. Should have barricaded the
door, should have fled with Sophie while I still had the
chance. Should *never* have forgotten the master key.

"Someone must think highly of you," said O'Reilly.
"These flowers, I mean."

As he twitched them toward Leigh, she retreated around
the table, one hand seeking blindly for support along the
back of a molded plastic chair. Outside was the world and
the silence. And inside, O'Reilly taking one more step nearer,
into the Coffin. He'd put on a checked workshirt, unbuttoned to the waist, and faded blue denims with the knees
scuffed white. Again, the familiar odors of alcohol and perspiration wafted from him.

"You're a very lucky girl," he slurred through a smile.

Behind him the light on the landing collapsed to dark. Another bulb increased to full brightness, flickered, then died
with the merest tick of sound, like a pin drop.

"Get out," she said. "I don't want them."

"But these are yours, there's even a note with them. Here."

Holding his ground, he laid down the spray on the tabletop. A handwritten card was pinned to it, but Leigh didn't dare look; she wasn't about to take her eyes from the landlord, as that would be just what he'd planned for.

"You've no business storming in here. You've no right to disrupt anyone's privacy like this."

"But I thought you were out, Leigh. I knocked, but all I heard was the television; when you didn't answer, I assumed you'd gone out and left it running."

In the small dark room there was nowhere to retreat to. She was pressed back between the sink and the two-burner hot plate, though O'Reilly was still only two paces in from the door.

"The meter ran out," she told him. "I need change. I wonder if you'd run down for some. I can't stay like this all night, can I?"

It would have been a brilliant scheme if he'd fallen for it, but instead his attention shifted to her suitcases. Though she couldn't tell his features from shadows now, she sensed his lopsided smile coming up, the slick movement of his tongue between his lips.

"You're packing," he said. "You're leaving me. Is it something I said or did?"

Just the way he was intimidating her now was enough. "If it's the rent you're worried about, don't worry, I mean to settle it with you," she said. "Sorry about the short notice. If that means you'll keep my deposit, you can have it with pleasure."

Now he was tutting, shaking his head like a patronizing older brother. "You've really got a bee in your bonnet, haven't you? And I would've thought you'd be pleased with these flowers."

"Don't want them," she said, so rigid her teeth were clamped. "Not from you."

"But they're *not* from me, that's all I meant to say. The florist delivered them earlier today. All I was doing was—"

She glanced at the table. The spray, all freesias and ferns and white chrysanthemums, was as far as the light from the window reached. Stapled to the cellophane wrapping was the message:

With all my love—now and forever
Stephen xx

Before she could fully digest it, O'Reilly took another leaden step forward. As he did so, the phone in the hall downstairs began ringing. Up here beneath the eaves it sounded miles distant, submerged in water. Leigh stood perfectly still, hardly daring to breathe until, after a dozen rings, it stopped.

"Someone must have answered it," she almost shouted. Only her fear kept her from fainting again, she was sure. "It could be for me—I'm expecting a call." She indicated the flowers. "From the young man who sent these. He's supposed to be meeting me here."

"If he's supposed to be meeting you, then why's he bothering to call? To say he's not coming perhaps?"

O'Reilly was almost entirely in silhouette now, and seemingly far larger than life, a fearsome presence blocking her escape route. As Leigh took a sideways step, meaning to dodge around him, O'Reilly came with her. In a room of this size, one quick maneuver was enough to shut her off from the door.

"What's he got that I haven't?" he demanded, his words thick with drink.

"I could give you a list," Leigh told him. "But for starters, he doesn't treat me as some *thing* to be gloated at and fantasized over. And he doesn't need booze to get up the courage to come near me."

"That's not for courage." O'Reilly wobbled awkwardly on his feet as he came closer. "That's company; it's to make up for being alone. It's the best painkiller I know."

There was a tremor in his voice that sounded like tears coming on. She knew the feeling; she'd had her share of emptiness too, but did he really expect sympathy from someone he was practically threatening?

"Please let me past," she said firmly. He was close enough now to touch her. "You're making me nervous."

"I don't mean to do that; only I can't let you go without letting you know how I feel. It isn't easy, you know, watching you come and go every day without saying anything, keeping it all locked up inside. I've tried making polite conversation, passing the time of day, and that's all I've been able to do to get close to you. Fact is, you remind me of someone I knew once; someone I was happy with and lost."

"Who?"

"Oh, no one you'd know. Her name was Stephanie; a girl with light shining out of her, was how I saw her, a natural grace, a love of life. Someone I suppose I've been trying to find again ever since."

"Someone you thought you'd found in me?"

"That's right."

"And Joannie before me. And Isabelle before her. And how many others besides?"

"I—" He fumbled; in the darkness, she heard his breath stop. "I don't understand."

But then, neither did she. "Tell me," she said, "What do you see in me that you also saw in Joan? We're so unalike. And Isabelle, for that matter. We couldn't all remind you of Stephanie. Did you kill them because in the end they didn't fit what you were looking for?"

There was sheer wonder and shock in his voice now. "Really, Leigh. I don't know *what* you're saying or why you're saying these hurtful things. Why are you doing this when all I mean is that I care? And who is Isabelle anyway?"

"The only thing I can't fathom," she said, "is *how* you did what you did to them. I saw enough of Joannie to want not to see any more. Even the police surgeons can't fathom what you did, but now's your chance to tell me in confidence, to tell me everything."

She must have been getting through, judging by the silence that followed. She'd either angered him deeply or baffled him by knowing so much. Perhaps that was why he'd temporarily forgotten to close off her path to the door. He was leaning away to his left, both hands gripping the sink to support himself. His strength seemed to have waned. His breathing had gained the heaviness of a smoker's wheeze, as if it were being slowly dragged from him.

It was her only chance. The lull, the crashing silence, only reminded her how deadly he was. He could strike at any time, without warning. With all the speed she could muster, she launched herself past his right shoulder toward the pale rectangle of light—the doorway—at the far side of the Coffin.

Even then, she was startled by how quickly he reacted. Both his hands were on her at once. Briefly the high, sweet smell of stale perspiration and beer washed into her face. He pushed her back by the shoulders, jamming her hard against the hot plate. The pans on the unlit burners rattled; the room shook as if the door had been slammed for effect. Something he'd knocked aside fell into the sink and smashed.

"What do you take me for?" the landlord was saying. "What do you mean, speaking to me as if I'm something you scraped off your shoe? Do you think I'm *completely* insensitive, that I don't even *know* the kind of things you and your friends say behind my back? I've feelings too, and don't you forget it. I've needs like everyone else, and if you think—"

He didn't have time to get the rest out. Before she knew what she was doing, she half turned to seize the nearest pan from the burners behind her—a heavy-bottomed frying pan as it happened—and hurled it toward him through the dark. She couldn't be sure where she struck him, but the impact was so great, the vibration still resounded through her arm seconds afterward.

O'Reilly tottered back, though still on his feet. From what she could see, he was clutching his shoulder. That was almost a relief; if she'd clipped him about the head, he wouldn't be living now, let alone standing. But with her relief came a new fear, a fresh understanding. Now that she'd shown him how much she knew, he was going to have to finish her. He wouldn't let her repeat it to anyone else. She'd left him no choice.

"Please," she heard herself say. "Let me go and I won't breathe a word, I won't tell a soul . . ."

At first she thought he was launching himself at her, since his arms were flung upward and out like a puppet's and his whole body seemed to be falling forward. It was only when he collapsed to the floor at her feet that she realized he was out like a light. Her shot with the frying pan had inflicted more damage than she'd thought.

It was then that she saw the object sticking out of his back, a glint of silver in the half-light. At first sight of that, her mind went blank; she couldn't make sense of it. She was about to stoop for a closer view when she noticed a figure at the doorway.

"Stephen?" she said. "Thank God, it's you! Thank God!"

Forgetting everything, she flung herself toward him, arms wide, tears threatening. Her face felt on fire, her body a mass of aches and pains. Her mind was a carousel running out of control. Stephen held her close, in the silent dark, until her heart slowed and her senses returned.

Then he said very quietly, "It's all right. I'm here."

"Oh, Stephen." Her heart went out to him in a surge that felt like the last of her energy leaving her. "Stephen, you realize what you've done? What *we've* done?"

"It had nothing to do with you. I'm to blame for everything."

She squinted through the murk toward where the landlord lay, though all she could see was a featureless hump. "Did you have to go so far?" she asked numbly.

"I overstepped the mark. I panicked; couldn't think. All I knew was that I had to stop him hurting you."

"He isn't moving. He isn't moving at all. Shouldn't we get help? Get someone to come?"

"It's too late for that," Stephen's words were spoken so coldly, they sounded unreal. "There's nothing we can do anymore."

Leigh felt a chill then that had nothing to do with the open window. In the darkness his features were unreadable. "But aren't you going to even look? Aren't you going to . . ." She tailed off. A lack of something in his touch made her draw back, startled.

"I love you, Leigh," he said quietly, and then she knew.

She'd overlooked it the first time, but now, at the table beneath the window, she again saw the note he'd sent with the flowers. *With all my love—now and forever.* Word for word, it was the message Graham had signed to his photograph. The handwriting, too, was Graham's. Except that there had never been any Graham, but there *had* been one lover and one killer, and this time his name was Stephen Roth.

"Leigh, let's make this a night to remember," he said.

· 16 ·

"Where is she?" Darren said.

Sophie looked up from her plate in the large, bright front room to see him leaning, breathless and red faced from running, against the doorframe.

"Where's who? Leigh, you mean? She's still at the Dene. She'll be over tomorrow, probably. Do you mind telling me what you've been doing?"

"Get moving and we'll go for her now," he said. He could barely speak for gasping for breath, since he'd run all the way from the Tech. The buses from there were too irregular to wait for. As he half dragged Sophie to her feet and downstairs, he said, "Is she meeting Stephen tonight?"

"Well, yes, that's why she couldn't come straight over." Sophie fished out her car keys as they reached the downstairs door to their apartment. "Is there a problem with that?"

"Yes, there might be. I think the problem is Stephen."

Not stopping to explain, he strode outdoors and away from her, toward where the Citroën was parked on Frederica

Road. Sophie invariably forgot to lock up, and he was already hunched in the passenger seat by the time she'd caught up and jumped in behind the wheel.

Waiting until she'd started the ignition, Darren continued. "Just now I saw Rob Young at the college. I had a set of Joan's negs with me, at a guess I'd say the last ones she took. On the roll were a half dozen or so candid shots of someone I couldn't identify—I decided to check them on the enlarger to see whether or not they were Graham—"

"There isn't a Graham," Sophie interjected. "That is, the face in the photos we handed in turned out to be some completely innocent poor bugger who lives miles away. I caught it on the news just now."

"Doesn't surprise me at all." Darren braced himself as she let in the clutch and jogged the car forward along the street. "Because the photographs Joan took were of Stephen Roth."

Sophie looked at him, nonplussed.

"Huh?"

"That's what I thought. What would *she* be doing taking these photographs—I mean, when you saw them projected down, you could tell how carefully focused and framed they were, as if they were shots she really cared about—what would she be doing taking photos of someone Leigh met only last week?"

Sophie threw up her hands, then remembered herself and grabbed at the wheel. "You're saying that Joan knew Stephen before? Couldn't she have taken the photos during those last few days?"

"Well, no. For one thing, Joan handed me the film to develop early last week; I'd forgotten I had it until today. For another, how could she could have known Stephen without the rest of us ever meeting him?"

"Maybe she was being protective. After all, she never allowed us to meet Graham . . ." The words had barely left her lips before it clicked, and she turned to Darren with an expression somewhere between wonder and terror. "Oh, Jesus," she said.

"That's right," Darren said. "We never met Graham because it was against Stephen's wishes; Stephen was the one who turned her into a recluse, because he was protecting himself from what he knew was going to happen to her."

"But what you're suggesting . . . Isn't that an awful lot to assume from a photograph she took? I mean, are you sure we're not misjudging Stephen here?"

"I would've said so, except for Rob Young. One glance at Stephen's mug shot and he identified Stephen as the one who took Isabelle Brooks away from him at some house party in Branksome Park the night she died. So if Stephen picked up Isabelle there on the rebound from Johnny Cross, and also knew Joan—"

The cogs were turning so thick and fast between Sophie's ears that she forgot to check traffic as she took the next turn. Fortunately, the nearest vehicles were held back by traffic lights.

She said, "If Stephen made such a point of avoiding us before, why did he come along to Horseshoe Common on the weekend? Why so suddenly go public?"

"*That* I don't know. Perhaps something has changed. Perhaps he knows something we don't and it doesn't matter to him now whether or not he's found out."

"Meaning what?" Sophie's eyes welled with sheer dread. "That Leigh will be the last?"

"I don't know. I don't know *what* I'm saying. But we've been watching all this through a smokescreen; a smokescreen Stephen put there. Now that it's clearing, I don't like what we're seeing one bit."

"My God, and to think she's there now, waiting for him to collect her!"

Sophie stabbed the accelerator so violently that she threatened to flood the engine. The streets flashed by like countdown markers toward Cavendish Road.

"We should have *known*," she was saying through her teeth, trying not to notice the Wimborne Road cemetery looming up on her left like an omen. "We should have seen this coming. Who was it said that hindsight was twenty-twenty? We should have realized those snaps of Graham were never Joannie's style: she couldn't have taken a happy-go-lucky photo to save her life; she'd have been striving for perfection."

"And now we know what the break-in at college was about." Darren pushed open his window to let in some fresh air. The inrushing air sounded relentless as high tide. During the night someone had broken open several lockers in the Art and Design department, though nothing of value had been claimed missing. "He must have been going through Joan's things for the film; he wouldn't have known I had it."

"And he broke open the other lockers so as not to draw attention to Joan's? To make it *look* like petty theft?"

"That's my guess. Here, go this way. It's quicker."

He was motioning right, instead of straight ahead for

Lansdowne. Fortunately the lights were in their favor. Long lines of vehicles sprawled back along three routes, engines revving, like a mass pile-up waiting to happen. As Sophie sped straight across the face of the traffic, the lights changed, the cars behind her drawing up sharply at the junction.

"God, will you hurry," Sophie whispered to herself and the situation in general. How long was it since she'd driven from the Dene in complete ignorance, leaving Leigh to await the unthinkable? Probably an hour, or longer, judging by the first signs of fading light, the orange glow suffusing the sky. Surely it was too soon for Stephen to have left work for the day. Provided Leigh was safe, there might still be time to phone the police and have Stephen picked up from Super-print.

For a moment Sophie was so lost in herself that she couldn't see why Darren was throwing up his hands in despair. The turning on their left into Cavendish Road was blocked. A double-decker bus had broken down across the junction mouth; the driver stood slightly aside from his vehicle, scratching the nape of his neck, while a man in a filthy boiler suit, a mechanic, hammered away at the engine. Several bored passengers stared blankly through the grimy windows. Others were disembarking to walk to the next stop.

Sophie had already slowed and was indicating to turn, but there was no way past the obstruction. Before she could react, Darren had shouted, "Damn it all!" and jumped out. Then he was running.

He never heard Sophie's reply; didn't give her time to suggest they take the next junction to Dean Park Road, working their way onto Cavendish from there. In the heat of the moment he hadn't thought ahead. Sophie watched him dodge out of sight around the bus, then slammed down the accelerator and sailed on.

So much for the quick route, Darren mentally kicked himself. If he'd kept his mouth shut, they would have been there already, and now he'd added time to their troubles.

It wasn't that the Wimborne Road approach was so much closer anyway; in the car it might have saved a minute at most. Now that he was on foot, Leigh seemed impossibly out of reach, far away to his left on the curving road that enclosed the cricket ground. If the road had been a clock, Silverwood Dene would have been at noon and Darren between seven and eight and barely ticking.

His legs were close to giving out. If he stopped or slowed, he'd never get moving again. The silence on Cavendish Road seemed remarkably large, but that was because his breath, his heartbeat, his steps were so loud. Each time his foot landed, the impact came like a slap at the crown of his head.

Please, he thought, let me arrive panting, unable to speak, making a fool of myself, who cares, as long as it isn't too late. Leigh should never have stayed another night at that place after Joan died; she must have been too preoccupied with Stephen to see anything clearly, to realize the Coffin was just waiting to live up to its name.

He was somewhere between nine and ten on the clock face when he heard the commotion ahead around the bend: all at once a clash of car horns, a screech of brakes, a muffled crack that might have been a collision or a gun going off. Right now he feared the worst. Passing Lansdowne Gardens, pushing himself up one more gear until his lungs felt constricted to the point of collapse, he reached the home stretch.

The first thing he saw was the Citroën, and Sophie motionless behind the wheel. She had parked, or been forced to stop, half on, half off the road, angling in toward the drive at Silverwood Dene. Slowing, Darren could see that the Citroën's near-side headlight had been shattered, the front grille slightly buckled. In the driver's seat, Sophie didn't so much as twitch. The engine was still running. His heart, keeping pace with his legs just seconds ago, now went haywire. Something between a sledgehammer and a knife went to work in his chest as he neared the car.

"Sophie?" he said, and then, "Sophie! Jesus, Sophie!"

He'd been prepared for almost anything but this. As he rounded the car, his eyes never left her. A knot of tension in his gut felt like the start of a rising scream. The engine was a constant low chug, a death rattle, the silence on Cavendish Road unbearable. Broken glass from the collision crisped under his feet.

Sophie never saw him. Her wrists were crossed and her fingers still intertwined on the wheel, her head bowed low. From outside looking in, there was no sign of blood. It wasn't until Darren reached her door, yanking it open, that she glanced up. Even then seconds passed before she recognized him.

The scream never reached Darren's lips; instead he gasped with relief.

"I thought," he said, taking her pale shocked face in his hands, "I thought you were—"

"You were very nearly right about that," she said. Then, "Did you see where they went?"

"Who?"

"Then you didn't. They must've taken off the way I came.

Could be anywhere by now." She touched fingertips to her temple, shook her head to clear the cobwebs. "Gave me a bit of a whiplash, but I think I'll survive. Come on, get in, don't just stand there."

"Wouldn't you rather I drove?"

"I'd rather we just get a move on." When he found the strength to budge and had jumped in beside her again, she said, "It's worse than I thought. Stephen isn't even bothering with the smokescreen now. As soon as he saw me turning in here, he sped out as fast as he could; almost took me apart in the process. You were right: something must have happened to change things."

"And Leigh? Was she with him?"

"Yes, but I couldn't be sure she saw me. There wasn't time to take anything in. Only—" She winced as she twisted to look behind her, then reversed out swiftly before speeding on toward Dean Park Road.

"Only what?" Darren wanted to know. "Only what?"

"Just an impression. It could have been something in Stephen's eyes, but everything happened so quickly, it's hard to be sure of what I saw; it must have been the way he came at me, so that I had to swing the wheel like mad to avoid him. It was as if he *wanted* the accident to happen—*wanted* to take Leigh with him there and then. Darren, if he cares so little for his own life, what chance does *she* have?"

· 17 ·

The killer flicked off the headlights, and darkness fell.

"Stephen, please," Leigh said wearily. "Don't make things worse than they already are."

Though it wasn't yet full dark, the road ahead looked uncomfortably vague with only the streetlamps for illumination. Shapes that might have been parked cars became, as they drew nearer, hedgerows or the shadows they cast. For the best part of an hour they had driven aimlessly and mostly in silence from one part of town to another while the sky reddened. Looking toward the horizon now, Leigh saw bloodstains spreading over the black land. She closed her eyes, wondering whether she would muster the strength to open them again.

At last Stephen switched the lights back to low beam.

"It isn't so effective while there's still daylight," he explained. "Once, many years ago, I drove to the country and kept the lights off and drove in total darkness until I felt myself panicking, unable to stand it a second longer. And you know what?" He waited for Leigh's prompt, which never came. "The first thing I saw when the lights came on was a tree rushing straight toward me. One more second and I'd have had it. I'd driven miles from the nearest road without knowing. To this day I still wonder whether what I felt then —the panic—was really the knowledge of death coming at me."

Whether or not he knew it, he was describing the way Leigh felt now. If she could only switch on some convenient light, make everything vanish, rewind events until she was back at the mailbox on Dean Park Road again, crushing the envelope in her hand instead of mailing it.

"I wish," she said, and stopped herself, biting her lip until the pain swelled through her numbness.

"What?" he said. "What do you wish?"

"I was going to say I wished we'd never met. But that wouldn't be true. Incredible as it sounds, I'm still—"

"Glad? But of course, so you should be. So am I. That's the whole point! Don't ever think I *meant* you harm. It was never like that, Leigh. Don't ever let anyone convince you of that."

But then, who would be there to convince her? She'd had her last contact with humanity: O'Reilly collapsing to the floor, knife lodged between his shoulders. She'd seen the last of her friends. Now, lulled by the smooth passage of the car over well-tended roads, she felt herself sagging and wondered whether death should be so peaceful, so easy. While Stephen took the next corner, she studied his profile, the Roman nose, the mildly rounded chin, and realized she knew his face as well as her own. Then why was he suddenly so unfamiliar?

"You deceived me," she told him. "You were lying to me all the time we were together. How could you if you really cared?"

"But I do care." They were driving along the Avenue, endless and tree lined, streetlights flicking between the uprights as they passed. "I only avoided the truth—I never exactly lied. Could I confess to you about Joan, for instance, or Isabelle or the others, without losing you?"

"The others. So many of them, I suppose."

"Truly beyond number," the killer said. "So many relationships coming to nothing. So often I've thought, This time it's for real; this time it's all there! And each time having to watch the good things slip away like sand through my fingers. So many sad memories, Leigh—but good ones too, let's not forget that! Let's never forget our good times, Leigh!"

No, she never would, but she couldn't allow herself to reminisce either. Just when she'd thought the good times were beginning, she was looking back, mourning their passing. The straight and broad road flashed toward her, bringing so many questions to mind, yet all she could say was, "Stephen? Who are you?"

There were several thudding beats of her heart before his response. "You mean you don't know?"

"Please don't," she said. "Please don't switch out the lights or play cat-and-mouse games. I've nothing left to give, no energy to fight with. Don't make me keep asking questions. You're a killer, I know. But what else are you? What gives you the right to put anyone through this?"

He was slowing the car to a crawl. Headlights washed

through from the rear; the vehicle behind sounded two sharp complaints on its horn and moved out to overtake.

"I'm the man of your dreams." The killer shrugged simplistically. "The name is Stephen Roth, and before that Graham Foulkes, and before that Michael Alton . . . Do you want me to go on, *ad infinitum?* I was everything you ever wanted, gentle and humble and caring, bringing you flowers and sharing your heartache; but for Joan I was something else again, all *her* heart's desires, partying all night, getting stoned, throwing caution to the wind. Every new lover makes a new man of me. I'm the Chameleon, Leigh, if you must know the truth. Just anything you want me to be."

Was he purposefully being difficult, or did he really believe what he was saying? Still edging the car slowly forward, he seemed to be scanning for somewhere to turn. The streets here were lined with white hotels. It was a wonder he could tell one from another.

"All the girls you've been with," Leigh said. "All the affairs that ended miserably. Are you saying you killed them all?"

"*Loved* them all. Death was a consequence, never an intention. I'd rather have sacrificed myself than seen so much suffering, so many lives going to waste. But I've never been able to entertain a relationship that meant nothing. I've always longed for something permanent; God, I've spent my whole long life down the ages pursuing that perfect thing. Do you know how it feels to destroy all you touch, and to loathe what you are, knowing there's no end to it?"

Please, she thought, don't do this. Please don't let it be happening. Stephen was either unhinged or utterly unreal, in possession of powers she neither understood nor wanted to. Deep in her mind a familiar mist formed, a vapor enveloped everything, thick as fallen snow. A hand lurched clear of it, clawing the air. The car scraped the curb and she jumped.

"Here, we turn here," the killer said suddenly. "This is our route to the beach."

So that was where he meant to end it. He hadn't been joking when he'd phoned this morning, suggesting a beach barbecue for two. She was almost past caring now anyway. The breeze from the open window couldn't revive her, and even if she threw open the passenger door to fling herself out, she'd only find herself spread-eagled in the street, unable to move.

"Where are we?" she asked, and Stephen replied, "Not far from where I first met Isabelle." That was as much as she wanted to know, but he'd already made the turn and had settled himself. "To this day I don't know how I allowed it to happen with her. I was still seeing Joan at the time. We met, and there was something between us at once: we fell for each other from the start. She wouldn't even have been there that night if she hadn't been running from some argument with her boyfriend. When I found her, she was killing time on the rebound with some poseur who meant nothing to her. But she knew I was for her, you could tell, the moment she saw me. The next thing I knew . . . we were together, and I was trying to blot Joannie out of my mind, not to feel guilty. And . . . it was over again. So quickly I was helpless to stop it. More sand through my fingers. I'll bet we didn't spend two hours together. Jesus. You don't mind me going over this, do you?"

Leigh said, "It hardly makes me feel better. But . . ."

"You'll want to know everything, though, won't you? You deserve to, after all I've put you through."

Casually and without thought, he reached to brush her cheek with the back of his hand. She recoiled automatically.

"Yes," she said. "Tell me everything, since I'm part of your plan. Just don't touch me again."

She could sense how much that hurt him. Even now, he felt for her deeply; but that was why he was dangerous, why his loving touch was poison.

"There was never any plan," Stephen said, idling the car along a quiet street of hotels and retirement homes half hidden by jutting cedars. "My only wish is that I could take back all the hurt I've given out. It's a blessing and a curse that love always came my way easily; girls like yourself gave me their hearts and souls without question. But the damage I've done, not wanting to, not able to stop myself . . . The way I treated Joan, for example, was so shabby. She knew I'd cheated, that I was being a bastard toward her, but nothing stopped her wanting me. We wept on each other's shoulders. I wrote her letters of apology and was forgiven. She never demanded much; not even that I be faithful.

"I learned about you from Joan, of course. She loved you too, loved all her friends; gave you such a glowing report, I felt I knew you even before I arranged our meeting."

"You arranged the party in Boscombe?" She was less surprised by that than saddened to hear how much Joan had cared. "Then you *were* the Graham Foulkes who worked at Apollo. You choreographed it all from there, in your own time. That's why the woman knew nothing about our get-together."

"Oh, Margery? You met her? A sad old case, don't you

think? So busy organizing clients' lives, she overlooks her own." He shook his head tiredly. "When I quit Apollo, I took a mound of their printed stationery and a hatful of clients' names and addresses. Obviously, to meet you, for instance, the Chameleon needed camouflage. That's why I invited the others to Sea Road. A strange brew, just names snatched randomly from a computer file, but they served a purpose. It was enough to know you'd be there."

She was beginning to feel like a puppet whose strings he'd been pulling. The sudden clear understanding of how he'd coordinated everything chilled her.

"I should have suspected something when the invitation arrived," she confessed. "It came too soon even for return mail; you hadn't bothered to stamp it. You wouldn't even have known I'd replied."

In the gathering dark the lights of his eyes burned fiercely. "Perhaps that was too hasty. The thing was thrown together so quickly, it was nearly botched. To be perfectly honest, I'd spent the night in Joan's apartment, then put the invitation on the hall stand when I left in the morning."

Jesus, to think he'd been *there,* directly below her, spinning his fatal web all night long! "And Joan? Did she have any idea about this?"

"Only so far as she knew the solicitations were going out through me, not the agency. Joan encouraged me to send them, even suggested I use your nickname, Mondrian. After all, she'd tried the agency herself, and—well, that's how *we* came together. She felt it might do you good. She never knew I intended to meet you myself."

"Why me, though? When you already had someone who

wanted you? When you didn't know the first thing about me?"

"Because you're you. You were searching for something special, and I never could resist that quality in anyone. Don't forget I already had a composite mental picture of you; partly through everything Joan told me, also because I know the kind of person who'll send off an Apollo application form rather than screw it up and throw it away."

"I did both," Leigh said. "Chances are we'd never have met if Joan hadn't insisted I give it a try."

They drove on without speaking until Stephen turned left onto a narrow, sharply dipping track road. Overhead, the thatched cover of leaves shut out the last light; and now she could hear waves rushing near and constant, as if rising along the lane to the car.

"We're almost there," he announced. A nervous edge had crept into his voice, a harsh irregularity to his breathing.

Leigh thought, This is where the world ends—at least for us. At least for me. Whether it was the sound of the sea or her own tired body calming her despite what lay ahead, she didn't know, but at last she had something to look forward to. He was going to put her out of her misery forever, this everyman killer named Michael or Stephen or—

"For a while we were sure another Graham Foulkes had killed Joan," she said. "A blond-haired, blue-eyed athlete."

He managed a laugh. "Joannie's ideal hunk. We used to joke about that."

"You signed and planted those photographs, then?"

"They were enough to throw everyone off the scent for a while. When I put them in her room, I was afraid, covering my tracks, not knowing how to handle what I'd done. You have to understand that, with all my heart, I've always tried to fight this thing, tried not to let it happen. When I lost Joan, I was devastated. I more or less went to pieces.

"I'd been working at Superprint only two or three weeks before those color snaps came in, mail order. To be fair, they could have been anyone; didn't really matter to me. It was easy enough to run off another set, give Graham a face as well as a name. I knew it wouldn't be long before the truth came out, but I needed to buy myself time."

She rounded on him with a ferocity that stunned even herself. "Time for what? For me? Time to make it happen all over again?" Briefly, her anger strengthened her. "How dare you pretend to be fighting it! Do you honestly expect me to believe you were mourning Joan and loving me at the same time? How could you even bring yourself to see me when you knew what you'd done?"

As the narrow, twisting lane ran out, the ocean rearing up grandly before them, she budged open the door on her side and stumbled outside.

Amazingly, she kept her footing, though the ground was all pebbles and dry, flaking turf. Stephen stopped the car alongside, leaving the lights on and the engine running, and began to climb out after her. As he did so, she backed away, ten or twelve paces, then turned and set off as quickly as she could.

They were somewhere on Alum Promenade, the sands in panorama before them, the horizon massing with scarlet clouds. To her left, a jetty extended partway out into the rising tide, and beyond, promenade lights joined the dots along the coast between Bournemouth and Boscombe. There were no illuminations over here, nearer Poole, except for the bloodshot sky and the mellow glow of Stephen's headlights on the sands.

Isabelle Brooks must have died about here, Leigh thought. Her body later washed around the bay to the harbor. Well, she'd have company soon. The killer had manipulated every small circumstance to bring Leigh to this point, where he wanted her.

"Leave me alone," she called over her shoulder. "Please, Stephen, leave me alone."

"Leigh, don't run. Don't be a fool."

She didn't dare look back. The sound of his footfalls behind spurred her on. But Stephen needn't hurry; her legs were barely carrying her forward, and he would catch her without trying if he wanted.

She dodged left, past two vacant viewing seats that faced out to sea, then toward the dozen or so stone steps descending to the beach. She didn't know what made her choose the sands—there was nowhere to hide or run there—but she was halfway down the steps before she sensed she was making a serious error.

Stephen was just behind her. Glancing back, Leigh saw him pass the benches and stride leisurely to the top of the steps. As he did so, he halted and raised both his arms, as if begging her to wait and surrender. But she'd surrendered too often already; she knew well enough how his touch, the warming sensation of those arms around her, changed things. Even though the dark blotted out his features, she could well imagine the pain she'd put there, the longing expression that proved he loved her. The distraction was only momentary, but enough to help her lose her balance. She was still five or six steps from the bottom when she felt her footing go. She fell the rest of the way.

The sand broke her fall, but she nevertheless managed to scrape a knee and go over on one ankle along the way. Everything went silent and gray for perhaps six or eight seconds. Then the pain made her conscious again, the worst of it in her stomach and chest, where the impact of landing had set off a rhythmic, deep-seated stabbing. At least she wasn't totally numb; right now, discomfort was the only thing telling her she was actually alive.

But not for much longer, she thought, when she realized Stephen was thumping down the steps toward her. He was crying her name, coming to sweep her up in his embrace, but she knew what that embrace had done for others. Thrusting out her hands, she tried to drag herself away across the cool sand. She didn't get very far. A crab would have been quicker, covered more distance. Stephen was there before she could move, helping her upright.

"Here. Let me. Does that foot hurt? See if you can take the weight off it."

Somehow he managed to manipulate her left arm about his neck, his right about her midriff. It was all over now. Her attempt to escape had been futile, her last gasp of life before giving in.

And now she felt herself surrender for the last time, knowing she hadn't the will or the strength to resist. He was walking her down the sands to the sea, perhaps as he'd done with Isabelle. Up on the promenade, the abandoned car's headlights blazed out of the dark, holding them in its spotlight. On the horizon a sea mist gathered, almost luminous beneath the red sky. In any other life this would have been paradise: the waves on the shore and the constant rushing sound of them, and Leigh in the arms of the man she adored. Not tonight though, she thought. Not now and not ever. Paradise had never been meant for her.

"All good things must end," he said quietly as they neared the water's edge.

They stood for a while, breathing in time with each other, arm in arm, with the water washing almost to their feet, then drawing steadily back inside itself.

"You really did love me, didn't you?" she said.

"Leigh, I still do, always will. Don't ever believe I lied about *that*. That's the horror of it, that we can't stay together, that I've taken so much life from you all, so much strength. That you've given so much away to me."

He was unhooking her arm from her shoulders now, collecting her hands in his, turning her around to face him. The light had improved, perhaps because of the glow coming in from the sea. Stephen was doing his best to force a smile.

"I hate good-byes," he said, gazing from Leigh toward the mist, his grip on her hands tightening. "Don't think too badly of me, will you, in spite of what I've done. Never tell yourself that I loved you less just because there were others before you."

She needed to tell herself something, though. With all her heart, she wished she could stop caring or wanting him, feel anger or loathing at what he was, anything that might help her face this. But she couldn't, and no wonder she'd been slowly wasting away ever since the night they'd made love; she'd always loved him unconditionally, and given herself over to him, expecting nothing in return.

Well, now the killer was taking the last of her. He'd done

the same to Isabelle, stealing her very life force for himself, emptying her out like a shell. He'd stolen again and again throughout the years. For Godsakes, she thought, let's get it over with, let's not prolong the agony. Her eyes were smarting, her heart racing wildly. The pressure inside her felt immense, as if she were about to scream uncontrollably. She'd always hated good-byes too, and could have done without one like this.

As the light from the horizon brightened, and a black wave rushing to the shore rose up as if stretching, she felt a change in Stephen like a temperature drop, a tremor running through him. Then the wave broke, and everything else fell into place.

"The Time has arrived," the killer said.

It wasn't a wave at all. At first it might have been, though she'd never seen a breaker like this in Bournemouth. Even when she told herself that what she was seeing was mist, it looked more like churning foam laden with gifts from the sea.

There were many shapes in the midst of it, none of which was easily identified. To her horror, she first caught sight of what looked like a white, bloodless corpse, picked clean by the ocean; a hand like the one in her painting reaching desperately for something to latch itself onto; a face that became almost recognizable before the mist covered it.

"What's happening?" she demanded, aghast. Stephen said nothing. Instead, he turned to her with a look of such sadness and awe, she felt herself beginning to understand.

"Dear God," she said. The shock was enough to steal her breath. She'd been asking the wrong questions, or at least forgotten to ask the one that mattered most: Stephen, what happened to the bodies? What did you do with Isabelle and Joan? What did you *do* with them?

Even without asking, she knew what his answer would be. She caught the fading look in his eyes, felt a surge of love coming from him like energy and life rushing back to her bones. For all that, her horror increased.

Stephen had done nothing with the bodies. Doubtless he'd been as unnerved as anyone the day they'd disappeared. More so, in fact, since only he could know and understand what the disappearance really meant. He'd always been accountable for the lives he'd stolen, and the certainty that one day he'd pay must always have haunted him. If that was what he meant by the Time, then this was the Time all right. His victims were returning to take back what he'd stolen. He must have known before bringing her here tonight. They'd driven to the beach to end it all, but not in the way she'd imagined.

"I love you," he managed, his voice sounding clogged and ancient.

"I love you too," she returned. This was it, then: the worst thing of all was about to happen. Unable to hold herself back any longer, she threw herself at him. As she did so, the mist reached the shore, washing over them.

Strangely, the first thought that struck her after that was an abstract one: that paradise and hell were two sides of a coin; you couldn't have one without the other. She knew this now because days ago—hours ago—Stephen Roth had been everything to her, the world, her life; and now he was crumbling. This moment should have been heavenly, but instead, death was smiling. As she flung her arms about him, the light inside the mist brightened sharply, and she felt his rib cage collapse inward.

Later, she couldn't be sure whether that was before or after the figures reached out of the mist for him. All she knew was that the waves in her painting had never been waves at all but patterns of swirling vapor, that as she stumbled backward in shock, she saw a man of perhaps eighty or ninety returning her gaze. In his eyes she still saw the love he felt; in her body she sensed new life, rejuvenation. Even as she looked, the years were multiplying on Stephen's brow, lines adding themselves to lines. Then she thought: Oh, stop, please stop, I'm stealing from him too, I'm destroying him too, oh, Jesus, please stop.

It was too much to bear. Suddenly she knew why her aches and pains were fading, her strength returning; and why his body was being picked clean by hands as soft as sea spray. She covered her mouth to muffle a cry, bit into her knuckles, drawing blood, feeling no pain. The figures were too numerous to count, too quick to identify. They moved about him nimbly, in absolute silence, in flashes of light like specters. One, Leigh saw quite clearly, lifted and wrenched his ragged hand from his arm as if it were clay. She knew that Joan and Isabelle were somewhere among them, claiming back what they'd lost. More hands reached; more parts of Stephen, small and large, were seized and taken. Oh please, she thought, or cried aloud, she couldn't tell which, please stop this. She stood, aghast, unable to help.

How could he have loved so many so completely? But then love was never static or fixed but constantly flowing, and couldn't be caged or nailed down. For Stephen Roth, that was the tragedy, that he had never been able to tame a power far greater than himself. When the last and greatest prizes, his eyes, were stolen from his face, Leigh twisted away, screaming for it to end.

God help him, she thought. And God help us all. And anyone who ever felt anything, who ever loved and lost anyone. It was all welling up in her, the pain and the rage, the sudden realization that Stephen was only a memory to her now. If she survived this, she'd live to curse her feelings, curse all those to whom love came so easily, who cruised though life never thinking about it. Wouldn't it be better to be numb, a zombie, feeling nothing at all, than to have to endure the hurt?

The mist was moving away along the beach. At first Leigh failed to realize she was free of it. She stumbled clear, gasping for air. There was no hint of life inside the glowing mass, no movement, no sign of the killer or his victims. In fact, what she saw was so insubstantial it was almost transparent. There was a sequence of strobing lights like camera flashes going off, an explosion of spray from a breaking wave, then silence.

She was drenched, her clothes clinging to her at twice their normal weight. The taste of salt filled her mouth. It was over, and in a minute she'd break down and weep and go on weeping indefinitely, but she mustn't let that happen yet, no matter how badly she hurt inside. She turned away, hugging herself to hold in the rising tears that felt like knives. On the horizon the redness softened to a gentle mauve hue as clouds parted: a perfect summer night sky just begging to be painted. Leigh took a mental picture of it—perhaps one day she *would* paint it—and, trembling, continued up the sands toward where Stephen's car waited, lights flaring. As she reached the steps, the headlights multiplied with the arrival of another vehicle. Doors slammed, silhouettes raced through the dark to meet her as she dragged herself to the promenade.

Please, she thought, let him still be alive. Let everything that's happened unmake itself, return to where it was before. She wouldn't mind the outcome as long as she could see him again just for a second. She knew this was a wild, impossible dream, but Stephen had always been that to her.

And the dream was over. Waiting at the top of the steps were Sophie and Darren.

"We looked everywhere for you," Sophie said. "You had us so worried. Thank goodness you're alive, Leigh."

Only up to a point, Leigh thought, and held out her hands to them both.

· 18 ·

Leigh stayed with Darren and Sophie until Sunday, when they returned to Cavendish Road to collect her things. Until then, the Coffin remained closed while police combed the Dene for evidence and interviewed residents at length. Only Leigh had been able to accurately describe the killer, though she'd pleaded ignorance when they'd asked what she thought his motives might be. In the end, unearthing a hoard of bootlegged X-rated videotapes among O'Reilly's possessions, they concluded the landlord had been mixed up with villains in the trade. His death had no connection with those of the missing young women, which still had the experts scratching their heads.

Why did Leigh feel she'd betrayed Stephen, even when she knew he would never be traced? Oh, he was out there all right, but not all in one place. He belonged to the rising tide now; he came in with the winds from the south, whispered through the leaves outside the open window of her room. He was lighter than air and couldn't be seen, but believing was not always seeing. Not as far as Leigh was concerned.

She was packing her canvases together and was about to follow Darren down to the forecourt when she thought she heard Stephen's voice. The net curtains fluttered, extending their shadow across the table, and outside, the birdsong became subdued. Strong winds had been forecast for later in the day, and at first that was what she thought she heard in the trees. But these sounds were not wind—more like partially formed words, a yawning vowel here, a sibilant hiss there.

I miss you, the hushed voice seemed to be trying to tell her.

"I miss you too," she returned, and then the moment was over, for Sophie was sweeping into the room behind her.

She stood with her hands on her yellow-trousered hips, surveying the empty space they were leaving. "You sure that's everything, Leigh? No socks stuffed with money in the back of your wardrobe? No old pairs of panties you've been using for dusters? Be sure now. We won't see this dump again, not if I've anything to do with it."

"That's all, I'm sure." But Leigh hesitated, expecting— she didn't know what.

Sophie came nearer. "Are you all right, Leigh?"

"As well as can be."

"Of course you are. Who wouldn't be, with me to look after them?" Smiling, she gave Leigh a quick, firm hug. "You're going to be fine, you know. You're going to get over this. It's a terrific healer, time, so they say. Listen, I don't know what happened out there that night, but you survived, you came through it. Whatever it was, I know it was devastating—anyone can see it's changed you. In a month or a year you might even feel like talking about it. But if not, re- member we're there and we understand."

"Thank you," Leigh said. "Thanks for everything, Sophie."

"Are you ready now?"

"More than ready."

Finished packing her paintings, Leigh thrust them into the crook of her arm and led the way out.

It was an arrangement that suited everyone. Leigh would keep the bed-settee at Darren and Sophie's until she found a place of her own, if that was what she decided she wanted. In the meantime she'd be sharing, thus lowering, their rent. And basking in the company she needed now more than ever. If she was ever going to get over Stephen, it wouldn't be something she attempted alone.

The building felt empty at last, after so much activity, so many gate-crashing reporters. As they came downstairs to the hall, the communal pay phone began ringing. Sophie twitched her nose at it and walked on. Leigh instinctively picked it up. Incredibly, as she did, she felt her heart lurch nervously. Did she really expect to hear his voice even now?

In fact it was her mother on the line.

"You were supposed to call me, my girl. I'm sure you've had something going on that's made you forget. Is everything hunky-dory?"

"We're in the middle of moving out, Mom. That's why—"

"We?"

"Sophie and Darren are helping. In fact, they're taking me in. It's the best thing all around, I'm sure. No, it hasn't ex- actly been hunky-dory, but now's not the time to explain."

"That's fine, as long as you know what you're doing. Keep

me posted. How's everything with this young man of yours?"

"It's—" She hesitated; there were a hundred ways to phrase it, none of which would make sense to a woman who judged every book by its cover. "It's over, Mom. For good."

Her mother sounded faintly amused. "Well, there you are then. It couldn't have been as special as all that, could it, for it to only last a week? You've done well to get it over with quickly, if you want my opinion; you can't let men get too firm a grip on your life, otherwise—"

"Mom, can this wait?" Leigh said sternly. She would have let the phone keep ringing if she'd known. The conversation was dredging it up again, inviting her to think about everything she'd been trying to bury.

"Yes, I understand," her mother said. "You're in the middle of moving. When you're settled, why don't I drop down and see you? We'll have that little heart-to-heart we've been promising ourselves."

Which heart-to-heart? Leigh wondered. But with as much enthusiasm as she could raise, she said, "Fine. That sounds . . . fine." Her mother had offered the same olive branch before she moved to Silverwood Dene, and nothing had come of it.

By the time she hung up, the distance between them felt greater than the four hundred miles it was. Hitching up her bundle of paintings, she walked down the hall, past the dusty mahogany stand—no mail today, thank you, God—and outside.

As always, the brightness outdoors startled her. It was another clear day, the clouds high, the sky's blue enriching itself like a color being mixed on her palette. The last of the journalists' cars had gone, thank God. This morning they'd exhausted her all over again with their endless intrusive questions and microphones forced toward her face, as if she hadn't already given enough of herself away. Now, across the forecourt, Sophie was climbing in behind the wheel of the Citroën while Darren reclined in the passenger seat, his left hand jutting from the window.

Leigh was halfway to the car when she remembered what she still had to do. She made a beeline for the dumpster, unraveling her painting of vapor from the tarpaulin as she went. It was no masterwork after all, but a too-accurate representation of something she'd lived through and now wanted to forget. The imprint of her hand on the paint surface was still visible, even after she'd fitted the canvas into the dumpster, which was eyebrow high. It looked as though the hand was clawing its way out again. She was reaching to push it farther down when she noticed a bird sitting on the dumpster's edge.

It was a canary, of all things. It must have escaped from a house nearby. While she finished what she was doing, it studied her intently, head inclined to one side, not even flinching when the painting dislodged something else in the dumpster, which toppled with a crash. Hope you find your way home, she thought; but beware the wild birds—you know what they'll do to you given half a chance. As she turned from the dumpster, the bird took off.

Leigh watched it go. For an instant, the world seemed to stop, the canary frozen in flight, a dash of impossibly bright yellow highlighted against the royal-blue sky. Then the breeze ruffled her hair and the bird was gone.

"Good-bye, Stephen," she said. "Wherever you are."

All good things must end, he'd told her. She couldn't see why it should be so. Someone should rewrite the rules one day. Sooner rather than later.

She picked up her step and headed back across the forecourt to where Darren and Sophie waited while the Citroën's engine turned over.